the misadventures of WiLLiE PLuMMeT

submarine SaNDWiCHeD

PAUL BUCHANAN & ROD RANDALL

The Misadventures of Willie Plummet

Cover illustration by John Ward.
Back cover photo by Ira Lippke.
Cover and interior design by Karol Bergdolt.

Copyright © 1998 by Rod Randall
Published by Concordia Publishing House
3558 S. Jefferson Avenue, St. Louis, MO 63118-3968
Manufactured in the United States of America

Library of Congress Cataloging-in-Publication Data

Buchanan, Paul, 1959-
    Submarine sandwiched / Paul Buchanan and Rod Randall.
    p.   cm. — (The misadventures of Willie Plummet)
    Summary: Willie explores his Christian values when the video camera on his model submarine uncovers poachers.
    ISBN 0-570-05042-1
    [1. Submarines—Fiction. 2. Inventors—Fiction. 3. Poaching—Fiction. 4. Christian life—Fiction.] I. Randall, Rod, 1962- . II. Title. III. Series: Buchanan, Paul, 1959- Misadventures of Willie Plummet.
PZ7.B97717Su 1998
[Fic]—dc21
                                 97-33070
                                    AC

3 4 5 6 7 8 9 10 11 12   09 08 07 06 05 04 03 02 01 00

To my wife, Leigh,
my first editor and best friend.

Contents

In Too Deep

An alligator sliced through the water in front of me. It had the tail of a serpent and more teeth than a chain saw. I glanced over my shoulder. The shore was 50 feet away. Bummer.

"Relax," I assured myself. "You're Willie Plummet, legendary adventurer, you can handle this." The cold water pressed against my rubber waders and gave me the chills. The early morning air was so quiet I could hear myself shiver.

I took a big step toward shore. Too big. The mud gave way. Water sloshed to the top of my waders, ready to pour in. I flung my arms in the air, trying to keep my balance. My feet slid in opposite directions. Time to panic. And to pray.

Doing the splits to death—what a way to go. But here I was, about to succumb to such a grisly fate. Not that getting munched by a man-eating reptile would be any better.

"Felix!" I yelled, feeling like the *Titanic* on its way down. "Throw me a rope! Quick!"

Felix sat on shore, tossing Lucky Charms in the air and catching them on his tongue. Adventure wasn't his thing, probably because he lagged behind in the growth department. He was short, with thin arms that he wrapped around himself in crowds when he wasn't busy pushing his glasses back up on his nose. But when it came to brains, Felix was hardly behind. He could solve equations in a split second.

As for me, I was a typical eighth-grader in build and brains. But my bright red hair was anything but typical. It made a raging bonfire look dull.

"Felix!" I shouted again.

"A rope?" he finally muttered, his mouth half-full of cereal. "You're dreaming. The fish can't be *that* big."

"It's for me!" I yelled. "There's an alligator after me."

"Sure there is," Felix laughed. "And Bigfoot has me in a headlock."

"I'm serious!" I screamed.

"Are you sure it's not the Loch Ness monster?" Felix called out. "Because that would be cool. Way cooler than some wimpy alligator."

"Hurry up!" I shouted, getting mad. But it was too late. A rush of water flowed over the top of my chest-high waders. Suddenly, a new threat entered the picture: drowning. The water felt like liquid ice as it soaked into my shirt and touched my ribs. I could feel my boots sliding farther apart. If I sank any deeper, water would fill my waders and hold me under.

"Felix! I'm not joking this time," I wailed. "There's something out here!" I pulled the waders as high as I could, trying to postpone the inevitable. I prayed for a miracle.

Another splash of water flowed into my waders. My feet slid wider apart. I yelled one last time. "Felix!"

Then I felt a tug on my suspenders. Something had hooked the canvas strap. It kept me from sinking. It began to pull me toward shore. I regained my footing and took a step into shallower water.

"Whoa," Felix exclaimed. "No wonder they call it Lunker Lake. For a sucker fish, you're a world record."

By now I realized what had happened. Felix had made the perfect cast, snagged the suspenders on my waders, and was reeling me in. Once I got to knee-deep water, I walked to shore.

"An alligator?" Felix questioned, his face full of doubt. "No offense, Willie, but what you saw was probably just a water snake. There aren't any alligators in this lake, or in this state, for that matter."

"This could only happen to me," I said, knowing Felix was right. "I stood out there for more than an hour and didn't catch one lousy fish. And now I'm soaked to the bone."

I peeled off the waders and dumped out a couple gallons of water. I took off my shirt and twisted it to wring out the water. When I put it back on, it stuck to me like glue.

"At least you *almost* caught a pretend alligator," Felix grinned. "Or did it almost catch you?"

"Enough already!" I shouted. "Unless you want to check out the alligator for yourself." I grabbed Felix's arm, ready to throw him in.

"Okay, okay," Felix conceded. He sat down and went back to his Lucky Charms.

"Fishing isn't supposed to be like this," I grumbled. "What happened to the trout lining up to bite my bait? In the past, catching fish at Lunker Lake was easy. Now they should rename it Junker Lake. Or Skunker Lake. Anything seems better than Lunker Lake."

I stared out at the water, wondering what had happened to the once-great fishing lake. "Maybe we just picked the wrong spot," I said.

"Maybe, maybe not," Felix offered, munching away. "But who knows?"

"That's a good question. Who knows?" I asked, mulling over some ideas in my head. "I mean really, who would know?" Then it hit me.

"Now what?" Felix asked.

"There's a bait shack at the far end of the lake. The guy there must know the hot spots. He has to," I explained. "It's his job."

"Forget it. You couldn't pay me enough money to go in there," Felix whined. "I've heard rumors about that place."

"What kind of rumors?" I asked.

"The kind that make you think, 'Forget it, you couldn't pay me enough money to go in there.'"

"Knock it off," I said. "Weren't you just giving *me* a hard time about the alligator?"

"That's because the alligator wasn't real, unlike the rumors about the bait shack," Felix reasoned.

"There's only one way to find out," I said.

After roping our fishing poles and tackle boxes to our bikes, we headed around the lake. I led the way. Felix followed behind at a distance.

When we entered the bait shack, I stopped short. No wonder Felix had heard so many rumors. The guy behind the counter freaked me out. He had bug eyes, wiry whiskers, and one long eyebrow that looked more like a flat Tootsie Roll than hair. His name tag read *Scrub*. But the ink looked smudged, like some of the letters had been erased.

"He looks like he could use a scrub," I whispered to Felix.

"No kidding. I wonder if Mr. Scrub is related to Leonard Grubb?" Felix asked, referring to the bully he had made a career of avoiding. "Scrub looks twice as mean as Leonard."

Scrub put down his magazine and looked me over with a smirk. "There's a rest room in back you can use."

"I don't need a rest room," I told him.

"At least not anymore, huh, sonny?" He chuckled softly, then returned to his *Four Wheeler* magazine.

Looking at my jeans, I clued in to his wisecrack. The ride around the lake had dried my clothes—at least most of the way. The bottom of my shirt and the top of my jeans were still damp. The dark area around my waist made it look like I had wet my pants.

Felix picked up on the joke and joined in. "Willie, maybe you should buy some diapers, just in case you have another accident." At that Felix and Scrub enjoyed a good laugh ... on me.

"It's just water from Lunker Lake," I pointed out. But it didn't seem to matter. Felix was doubled over laughing, and Scrub's face was so red he looked sunburned.

I figured the only way to break this up was to change the subject—and soon. "This isn't what it looks like. The truth is, I wouldn't have soaked my pants if the fishing in this lake didn't stink."

Scrub quit laughing and gave me a hard look. "Maybe it's your bait."

When I explained that we had tried worms, cheese, and even Lucky Charms, Scrub shrugged and suggested that we change spots. When I told him we had tried that too, he turned angry and grumbled something I couldn't understand.

"Thanks anyway," I said, backing toward the door. I wanted to escape before he turned his anger on me.

"Where do you think you're going?" he asked, glaring at us suspiciously. Then he motioned Felix and me closer without saying another word.

②

The Lunker Lake Escape

I edged toward the counter. Felix followed. Scrub looked from side to side, as if furious and nervous at the same time. "Maybe you should try someplace else, like Pinnacle Lake. I guess they're doing pretty good up there," Scrub said through clenched teeth.

"But Lunker Lake is known for huge fish," I countered.

Scrub leaned over, his yellow teeth close to my face. "Have you caught any huge fish?"

"No," I admitted.

"Have you *seen* anyone catching huge fish?" he rumbled.

"No."

His eyes narrowed. "Take my advice. Try Pinnacle Lake. Lunker Lake ain't what it used to be. There's nothing here for you to catch, so forget it." With that Scrub returned to his *Four Wheeler* magazine, at least sort of. As we left, he kept an eye on us. Even after we got on our bikes, I could see Scrub in the window, watching us ride away.

"What's *his* problem?" I wondered out loud as I ped-dled. "And what's with his name? *Scrub*. That's not a name, it's a verb."

"I tried to warn you," Felix said. "Oh well, at least we survived our visit to the bait shack. And we got a hot tip for next time."

"Is that what that was?" I asked.

"What do you mean?"

"It doesn't make any sense. Why would Scrub drive away customers by sending them to a different lake?"

"He was just trying to be helpful," Felix suggested.

"Scrub didn't sound too helpful. He sounded both-ered. Especially when I pushed him about Lunker Lake. What's going on around here anyway?"

As we rode, the lake filled the canyon to our right. It looked as gorgeous as ever—at least on the surface. The story beneath the surface wasn't so hot. "If only we had a way to explore the lake," I said, thinking out loud again. "I'd love to see where the fish are hiding."

We turned onto the dirt road—our shortcut to Glen-field. The turns were sharper and the cliffs steeper than the highway, but it saved time. And except for a few off-road vehicles, we didn't have to worry about cars.

Riding along, the faint hum of an engine echoed through the hills behind us. With each turn, it got closer. "What is that?" I asked.

"A 5-liter V-8 with automatic transmission," Felix said without hesitation. "It's standard in most full-size pickups."

We picked up our speed, but we could still feel the truck barreling down on us.

"Felix, stay to the side of the road," I cautioned.

The road wound around a bend. We peddled faster, hoping to reach our turnout before the truck caught us. Sagebrush and jagged rocks covered the hillside—the kind of ground that turns you into a human scab if you wipe out.

The truck's engine roared louder. Any second it would flatten us like bugs on a windshield. I listened for squealing brakes. Nothing. My legs felt like rubber bands. They were peddling as fast as they could. My red hair whipped like a torch in the wind.

Another hundred yards to the turnout. From there we would jump off the dirt road and cut through the trees to Glenfield. I peddled faster, praying we would make it. Even an off-road vehicle couldn't follow us on the trail.

"Keep going, Felix!" I yelled.

"We'll never make it!" he shouted back.

I could see the dirt path. Only 50 feet. Forty. The engine revved and burned. I chanced a look back, but the vehicle was hidden by the bend in the road. Did the driver see us? Did he even know we were here?

At the turnout there was a jump to the trail below. At this speed we would fly a mile, but we couldn't slow down. The dirt road was too narrow for the truck to pass without sideswiping us both.

Twenty feet. Ten. The engine roared right behind us. We could feel the heat. It seemed to push us forward.

Five feet. Three. Two. One. Now! Felix and I launched off the jump and soared like birds. Turkeys, actually. The truck heaved around the next turn, leaving a cloud of dust and gravel in its wake.

We landed hard. For a moment I tasted how my great-great-grandfather, Jedediah Plummet, must have felt when he built those first flying machines. My bike tire hit a rock and I flew over the handlebars. My mouth became a plow as it furrowed through the dirt. I didn't stop until my head met a boulder. By the time I staggered to my feet, the truck had roared out of sight.

Felix was on his back, staring at the sky. His bike was in a tree. "I guess we showed him."

"Yeah," I said, licking the dirt from my teeth and rubbing my head. "He must have *really* been afraid of us to leave that fast."

The rest of the way home we couldn't stop looking over our shoulders, wondering if the death truck would return. The fact that Scrub was reading a *Four Wheeler* magazine kept coming to mind. "I bet it was Scrub," I told Felix. "He told us to find another lake, and that was his way of making sure. If only we knew why he was so determined to keep us away from Lunker Lake."

At home, my mom bandaged the cut on my head. It felt like someone had taken a sledgehammer to my brain. "You can't get this bandage wet," she told me. "You'll have to wear my shower cap when you clean up."

"Why do I need to clean up, Mom? It's Saturday, and you know I'll just get dirty again." Reason always seemed to work with my mom.

"You smell like a fish and you're covered in dirt, Wilbur," my mom replied. "Besides, your dad got a shipment in at the store and he needs your help unpacking."

"Lucky me," I grumbled as I climbed the stairs. Because the shower cap was in my parent's bathroom, I decided to shower there. But after undressing and putting on the cap, I realized there was no soap. What a pain. Rather than put my clothes back on, I threw on my mom's pink bathrobe and headed for the other bathroom.

On my way down the hall, a sound caught my attention. It was coming from my bedroom. *Now what?* I wondered. *Who's in there? And who closed my door?* After the death truck incident I was feeling a little skittish.

I approached the door, listening intently. A soft whirring sound came from inside, then footsteps. My brother and sister, Orville and Amanda, were both out, so it couldn't be them. My dad was at work. And if it was my mom, why would she close the door? Time to find out, I decided. I grabbed the doorknob and flung the door open.

"No," I screamed. I shuddered in horror. My legs went limp.

In front of me, just inches from my face, was the one thing a junior high guy—wearing his mom's shower cap and pink bathrobe—fears most. A video camera! And the blinking red light could only mean one thing: It was recording!

A Video Voyage

"It's show time, Willie!" a familiar voice announced. *Phoebe* held the video camera against her eye. She was in fourth grade and lived next door. She had freckles, green eyes, and short brown hair with bangs.

"What are you doing in here?" I demanded.

"Filming your room," Phoebe replied with a smirk that said I was dumb for asking. "Your mom let me in. She said you'd still be in the shower."

"Shut that thing off," I said, lunging for the camera. But my mom's bathrobe bunched like a rope around my legs. I tripped to the floor.

Phoebe jumped past me and into the hall. "Relax, Willie. You'll be glad I caught you on film. My school project is to make a video of someone I admire. That's you, of course."

"Of course," I moaned. Phoebe tended to stick to me like permanent marker. This was just one of many times she had made her admiration known.

"Phoebe, no offense, but this sounds like a nightmare. Every time I do something stupid, you'll be right there with your camera."

"Not *every* time you do something stupid. I don't have that much videotape. I would need two cameras. And a film crew. Maybe two film crews. And a production company. Maybe two …"

"All right already. I get the point," I said, content to just lie on the floor and hide under my shower cap.

"Come on, Willie. I won't be a pest. Besides, I'm dying to try out my parents' new video camera. Look how small it is. This thing can go anywhere."

"Anywhere?" I asked, looking up. Suddenly my scheming mind went berserk. I thought of my frustration at Lunker Lake. *If only we could see what's really happening underwater.*

"Look at it," Phoebe said. "It weighs only three pounds."

Phoebe handed me the video camera. It was no bigger than my hand. "Phoebe, is this thing waterproof?"

"I don't think so."

"Too bad," I said, looking through the viewfinder. "But we can make do."

"What are you talking about?" she asked.

Time to pour on the Willie Plummet charm. I put my arm on her shoulder. "Phoebe, my wonderful little admirer, can I borrow this camera for a few hours?"

Looking up, Phoebe batted her eyes. "Whatever for?"

"Let's just say there's a project I need to accomplish."

"You mean like the school project *I* need to accomplish, Mr. Camera Shy?" She offered a coy grin.

What can I say, she had me. "Okay, I'll accept my role as the person you admire."

"Then I guess it's all right if you borrow the camera, as long as you bring it back before dinner."

I extended my hand. "Phoebe, you've got a deal."

She shook hands with me and walked out of my room. I could hear her whistling as she walked down the stairs. Before jumping in the shower, I called Felix to explain my plan.

An hour later Felix and I met in the lab. The lab was really the back room of my dad's store. We called it "the lab" because it sounded cooler than "the back room of my dad's store." It was also where our experiments came together.

As I'd explained to Felix on the phone, we needed to convert a model of a Goodyear blimp, a remote control battleship, and some spare appliance parts into a submarine capable of housing Phoebe's video camera. The fact that my family owns Plummet's Hobbies definitely would help. There were enough gizmos and gadgets on hand to create just about anything.

On this project, Felix provided the technical expertise and I offered the verbal support. Comments such as "What's taking you so long?" and "Aren't you done yet?" were a few of my specialties. For some weird reason, though, Felix couldn't appreciate an encouraging remark if it tickled him. Suddenly, he grabbed my collar. "Willie, either you give me some space or I'm outta here."

"Touch-eee," I complained. Heading to the front of the store, I helped my dad unpack and stock the shipment of model glue.

That's when Samantha stopped in. Along with Felix and me, she completed our adventurers' triangle. Like the Bermuda Triangle, suspicious circumstances tended to arise when the three of us started scheming. At least that's what our parents said.

"I'm beat," Sam moaned, resting her arms on the front counter.

"From what?" I asked.

"Flag team. The fall invitational is next week. I've been twirling flags for three hours a day just to get ready."

I laughed. "How tough is twirling a flag? That's like getting a sideache from watching TV. You should be doing something cool, like baseball. Now that impresses people."

"Watching TV, huh?" Sam flexed her arm so I could feel her biceps.

I lifted my eyebrows in amazement. "Wow. Pretty soon you'll look like an Amazon ape girl."

Sam cringed. "Since when do apes come from the Amazon?"

"Since you tried out for flag team."

"Spazz down, Willie. You sound just like my dad."

"It's just that you're such a good athlete," I said. "I hate to see you waste your time on ..."

"It's not a waste of time," Sam argued, sounding bothered. "Where's Felix?" Maybe he won't be such a dweeb."

"Forget about Felix. He's in the back room finishing our project." I explained to her everything that had happened at Lunker Lake.

"Are you sure we need a video submarine?" Sam asked. "Couldn't we just have the Skyrunner 1000 fly over Lunker Lake with a camera?"

"Not funny," I said, remembering the misadventure caused by my flying machine. The people of Glenfield, not to mention the Air Force, confused the Skyrunner 1000 with a UFO, which led to all kinds of problems. But that's another story.

"So when will Felix be done?" Sam asked.

"Any minute, I hope. I'd still be helping him, but he got ticked off when I tried to offer a little motivation."

"Don't believe him, Sam." Felix stood in the doorway to the back room. "If you guys want to see the Video Sub, it's ready."

We made our way to the lab. My dad even took a break from the cash register to have a look. He left my older brother, Orville, in charge, which was an adventure all by itself.

Sam looked the submarine over. "It looks like a cross between a torpedo and a toaster, minus the cord."

"I'm not sure it looks that good," Dad added. "So where do you put the bread?"

I shook my head. "Dad, it's not a toaster."

Sam wouldn't let up. "When the fish see this coming, they'll be scared to death."

"Either that or they'll die laughing," Dad continued.

"Willie designed it," Felix said and shrugged. "I just made it work."

The submarine was about two feet long and shaped like an overweight missile. The shell was made from gray plastic and stainless steel, except for the front window.

Felix grabbed the remote to give us a demonstration. When he moved the lever forward, the propeller accelerated. When he moved the lever backward, the propeller turned in reverse. Other knobs moved the rudder and controlled the speed.

"What about Phoebe's camera?" I asked.

"It's already installed. You can see it through the clear plastic in front." We looked through the window while Felix continued his explanation. "All I have to do is open the leak-proof hatch to hit the record button. Then it's surveillance time."

That was enough for me. The hottest fishing holes at Lunker Lake were as good as ours. Our brilliant triangle had done it again.

One hour later, Felix and Sam and I were standing on the shore of Lunker Lake, ready to test our invention. Our plan was simple. We'd walk along the shore with the Video Sub in the water next to us. It would record everything in its path.

My job was to carry the sonar imager Felix had made from an old fish finder. It would monitor the exact location of the submarine. Felix would steer the Video Sub with the remote control.

Sam's job was to keep accurate records of our time and location. Then when we watched the videotape at home, we'd not only see the fish, we'd know just where they were hiding. I would have preferred a "live" viewing so we could see the fish as the camera recorded them, but we didn't have the equipment for that.

As soon as Felix placed the Video Sub in the water, he started getting nervous. "If it doesn't work, how will we retrieve Phoebe's camera?"

"It'll work. Don't worry," I told him. "Launch it."

Sam shrugged when Felix looked to her for support. With nowhere else to turn, he opened the hatch,
pressed the record button, and set the Video Sub adrift.
Working the remote, he maneuvered the submarine to
about 30 feet from the shore, then dropped it 10 feet
down. I monitored the sonar, and Sam noted the time
as we began to move along the bank.

"It's working perfectly," I said. The blips on the
sonar screen moved in conjunction with our steps. "I
can't wait to see what it's filming."

Sam recorded every landmark we passed and the
exact time. Hangman's Tree at 6:23 minutes in the
water. Bird Rock at 11:08 minutes. "Like clockwork,"
she announced.

As we trekked along the shore, I heard the faint
whirr of a distant engine. "Not again," I moaned,
remembering the truck that almost had mowed us
down earlier in the day.

"What?" Sam asked.

Taking my eyes off the sonar screen, I checked up
and down the road that wound around the lake.
"Remember the truck I told you about?"

The engine grew louder. And closer. "Oh, yeah,"
she said, cringing.

"Not, 'Oh, yeah,' " Felix added, his face tombstone
white. "*Oh, no!*"

The truck rumbled on the other side of the bend.
We dropped to the ground, hiding behind the reeds at
the water's edge.

"*Scrub*," I fumed, remembering how he had looked in the bait shack with his wiry whiskers and long Tootsie Roll eyebrow. His face had "guilty" written all over it.

"He must have seen our bikes," Felix whispered.

"And returned to finish what he started," I added.

Crouching low, we waited, trying not to breathe. Felix was so freaked out that he dropped the remote and lost control of the submarine. His hands were shaking so badly that when he tried to pick up the remote, he dropped it again.

Then I noticed something on the sonar screen. "Oh, no," I whispered. Felix and Sam joined me in staring at the blinking green dot on the screen. The Video Sub had stopped moving.

Sonar Surveillance

With the truck nearly upon us, the Video Sub floated to the top of the lake.

"Felix," I grumbled, still hiding behind the reeds, "if the driver sees that ..."

Just as the truck arrived, Felix grabbed the remote and took the submarine down again. "He couldn't have seen it," he assured me.

I had my doubts and waited for the truck's giant treads to roll over our heads. But I was wrong. Soon the truck's engine faded in the distance. By the time we stood up to take a look at the vehicle, it was gone.

"Great," I complained. "That's twice now and we still haven't seen it."

"Then how do you know it was the same guy?" Sam asked.

"The engine," Felix replied. "It was the same V-8 automatic. The timing's off and one of the spark plugs needs replacing."

With the truck no longer a threat, we continued walking around the lake. I watched the sonar screen to make sure the Video Sub moved in sync with us. Sam recorded key landmarks in the log.

"How's it doing?" I asked.

"Just fine," Felix replied.

"This is better than the movies," I said. "I can't wait to see all those trout and bass captured on video." I imagined massive largemouths, hungry for my baited hook. I could practically see the new lake record mounted above my fireplace. Maybe the mayor would want to have his picture taken with me. I'd try to fit him into my schedule, but with all the other press interviews, he'd have to wait his turn.

"Willie, pay attention!" Sam warned.

"What? Huh?" I muttered, snapping back to reality.

"The sonar," she said, pointing at the screen with her pencil. "It's not moving again. The submarine must be stuck."

Felix glanced at the blinking dot on the screen. "She's right. And this time it's not my fault." He used the remote to put the Video Sub in reverse. At first the sonar dot didn't move, then it slowly backed across the screen. "Whew," he sighed in relief. "That was close. I thought it was stuck."

"It must have hit a rock or something," I suggested. "Try moving ahead in deeper water."

Felix used the remote to turn the submarine. Once it was farther out, he attempted to cruise parallel to the shore again.

"So far so good," I assured him, watching the blinking dot on the sonar.

But our success didn't last. Moments later the Video Sub stopped again. We worked the submarine back and forth for the next 20 minutes, but no matter where we tried to direct it, it kept getting hung up.

"What's out there?" I wondered out loud.

Watching the sonar carefully, Felix noticed that the Video Sub didn't stop right away. Instead, it gradually quit moving. "It's not just a tree stump or rock, that's for sure," he pointed out.

I shrugged. "We'll have to bring it in and relaunch it farther down the shore."

Sam looked at her watch. "When did Phoebe want the camera back?"

"By dinner," I replied.

"In that case, it's time to go," Felix announced. He directed the submarine straight to shore and scooped it up. "Besides, I'm ready to see what we caught on film."

I agreed, and we turned to leave. Then a twig snapped behind us. I spun around, still a little freaked out by the truck that had tried to run us off the road. But nothing was there. A few branches swayed in the breeze. That was all.

Without saying a word to one another, we picked up our pace. Apparently I wasn't the only one freaked out by the truck attack.

Another sound came from behind us. Dry pine needles crunched on the ground near the spot where the submarine had been stuck. I whipped around and thought I saw a figure slide behind a tree. "Someone's back there," I whispered.

"It's probably just a deer," Sam reasoned.

"With long sleeves and a hat?" I asked.

"So it's a well-dressed deer," Felix added. "A spiffy deer is a happy deer. Now let's keep moving."

Believe me, we did. Our speed continued to increase. We moved like race walkers, but so did the footsteps behind us. We tried stopping, but the footsteps stopped too. We rushed ahead, knowing someone was behind us.

When we reached our bikes, we loaded up our gear and headed out. I listened for the same loud engine and monster tires to come tearing down the road, gravel and dirt flying. We peddled hard, rounding turn after turn. Soon we reached the dirt trail and jumped for safety.

Then an engine turned on. Loudly. Close by.

"The same truck?" Sam asked Felix.

"I think so. Definitely a V-8." We stopped our bikes and hid behind the nearest bushes we could find. Moments later a green light-utility truck drove by nice and easy.

Sam took one look and busted out laughing. "You were afraid of him? The ranger?" She laughed even louder. "Yeah, he's *real* scary."

"Actually, he's the game warden," Felix pointed out.

"No wonder you were scared," Sam said, still cracking up. "He might send all the chipmunks and bunnies after you."

"That's not the truck that chased us down this morning," I said, feeling my face turn as red as my hair. Felix nodded in agreement.

"Sure," Sam teased. "Whatever you say."

Peddling the rest of the way home with the evening breeze on my face, it was worth feeling embarrassed just to be safe. I said a quick thank-You prayer. The sunset filled the sky with purple and orange, and for a moment I could appreciate the beauty. Then I remembered the videotape we had shot and couldn't help but think something on there might surprise us. We cruised downhill until we reached my house. It had never felt so good to be home.

Then I saw my mom and everything changed.

She stood on the front porch, fuming. "Where have you been?" she demanded.

"Making a surveillance tape," I told her, feeling proud of myself. "With our custom-made, remote control Video Sub."

She wasn't impressed. "Phoebe called three times. She needs her camera." Felix and Sam waited at my house while I jogged next door.

Phoebe glared at me as I approached. "Our agreement was that you would bring the camera back *by dinner.* So far all I have for *my* video project is you wearing a pink robe and a shower cap that don't even match. No offense, Willie, it's a funny shot and all, but it's not very admirable."

"Phoebe, listen, I need your camera to play the tape we just shot. Give me until tonight, then I'll do something admirable that you can record. I promise."

"Okay, but I wouldn't break that promise if I were you," Phoebe said, still glaring at me. "Imagine what would happen if the tape I shot of you fell into the wrong hands, say Leonard 'the Crusher' Grubb's, for instance."

"You wouldn't ..."

"See you after dinner, Willie." Phoebe grinned as if she owned me, then closed the door in my face.

Walking back across the lawn, I stopped in my tracks. I had the feeling I was being watched. Normally that was no big deal because Phoebe watched me all the time, but this was different. I looked all around, but I couldn't see anything out of the ordinary. After a few more steps, I paused to look again. Nothing.

Back at my house, Felix and Sam were waiting. We headed for the family room and hooked up the camera to the TV.

"Ready?" I asked, after rewinding the tape.

"We've been ready," Felix said. I pushed the play button and sat back, ready to enjoy an underwater journey on videotape.

"What's wrong with it?" Sam asked. So much for my journey. It looked like someone had dropped the camera in a mud puddle.

"Just be patient," Felix said. "It will get better."

He was right. The visibility gradually improved. As the submarine cruised away from shore, where the water was dirty from runoff, strange aquatic sights came into view. Underwater plants clung to the bottom and swayed toward the surface. Minnows glided along. Soon we spotted two skid marks in the mud, sliding off in opposite directions.

"What are those?" Sam asked.

"Didn't you hear?" Felix replied. "When the fish wouldn't bite this morning, Willie did the splits in protest."

Sam looked at me and grinned. "Did it help?"

"No, it hurt."

"Then maybe you need a sport that will loosen you up, like flag team, for instance."

"Funny," I said, staring at the videotape, not wanting to miss a frame. It was like watching one of those undersea movies on the Discovery Channel, only better because we'd made it.

Finally, Felix broke the silence. "I know it's a fresh-water lake, but it still feels like any moment a tiger shark will rise from the depths, open his jaws, and chomp the Video Sub to shreds." Just as Felix said that a minnow bumped the submarine's window, eyed the camera, then swam away in a panic.

"That's some tiger shark," Sam teased.

I laughed with her. "As long as it leads us to the big ones, I'm happy."

When the submarine turned to cruise parallel to the shoreline, Sam compared her logbook with the time on the video. "At 6:23 minutes elapsed, we should see the submerged roots of Hangman's Tree." We watched as more plants and small rocks came into view. Then, right on schedule, we saw the old tree stump.

I expected to spot a hog of a trout resting in the tangle of roots, but no trophy fish appeared. The water was so empty it was eerie. In fact, other than a few guppies, not one fish swam into view.

"Something's not right," Felix admitted, shocked by the absence of trout and bass.

Sam kept an eye on her notes. "Ten more seconds and Bird Rock should pass by on the left." It did, and we took some gratification in knowing that our system had worked as it should. Now if only the camera would locate some fish. But it didn't. As Sam read off a few more markers, the water on the video was as vacant as ever.

"This is the most boring undersea special I've ever seen," Felix said. "We can forget about that million dollar offer from the Discovery Channel for our tape."

"What's the next big landmark?" I asked.

"There isn't one," Sam said. "In 15 seconds the Video Sub hits the wall."

With my focus on the fish, or lack thereof, I had forgotten about the mysterious barrier that had stopped the submarine. I watched with anticipation, wondering if the barrier would explain what had happened to all the fish.

Felix was just as captivated. He leaned on his knees, his mouth open, his eyes glued to the screen. Even Sam got into it. She edged closer to the TV set, ready to see the mystery of Lunker Lake unfold.

Edible Evidence

"What's wrong with your TV?" Felix asked. A grid began to appear in the background of the picture.

I stared at the video, wondering what was going on. Soon we could see movement in the water ahead. Flashes of silver twisted against the blue backdrop.

The Video Sub continued to motor forward. The flashes of silver took shape. We squinted at the TV, trying to decipher the pattern in the background.

Felix was the first to figure it out. "I don't believe it," he said, stunned.

"What? What?" Sam and I asked. Before Felix answered, we figured it out for ourselves. The scene was horrible. Dozens of trout and bass hung by their gills, trapped. The grid was a commercial fishing net. Some of the fish were small, others lunkers. The net stretched from one side of the TV screen to the other, making it as wide as it was deadly.

"No wonder the submarine stopped," Sam said.

"No wonder I can't catch any fish," I added, feeling sick with disgust.

The submarine continued to cruise ahead until a trout was sandwiched between the front window and the nylon net. We watched as the Video Sub drove into the net again and again, traveling the length of it in its search for an opening.

"The Video Sub never stood a chance," Felix admitted.

"Neither did those fish," I said. "No wonder Scrub wanted us to get lost. He's poaching all the fish from Lunker Lake."

Sam tried to be diplomatic. "You don't know that he's the one who strung that net."

"I know he almost tried to kill us with his truck," I countered. "Wait 'til you see his face. There's guilt written all over it."

Felix looked around suspiciously, as if it wasn't even safe to be in my house. "Now what?"

"We need to call the police," Sam said.

Hearing the word *police* brought my dad into the room. He watched the video and listened to our story. "I wouldn't start with the police," Dad said. "For all you know the Fish and Wildlife Department is doing some kind of research up there. That could explain the net."

I remembered the green truck. "What about calling the game warden?" That sounded good to everyone, including my dad. He left us to our video so he could finish some yard work.

Felix and Sam gathered around while I made the call. After five rings a machine clicked on. It explained that the office was closed and gave the hours to call.

"Now what?" Felix asked.

"We call again tomorrow after church," I said. Felix and Sam were fine with that, as long as the tape stayed with me.

The footsteps in the woods suddenly came to mind. I wondered if keeping the videotape was such a good idea. Maybe it would be best to keep the tape as far away from me as possible.

Getting ready for bed that night, I felt uneasy. If the poacher went that far to catch fish, how far would he go to get our videotape? I kept hearing those steps behind us. Had someone followed us? Would he try to break in tonight just to get the tape?

"Mom," I yelled, pulling open my dresser drawer, "where are my pajamas?"

"In the dryer," she yelled back. "If you want them, go get them."

Something told me I should, but I didn't feel like going downstairs and into the garage. Searching the back of my drawer, I found a pair of Winnie the Pooh pajamas my grandma had given me for Christmas last year—sometimes she forgets how mature I am. I decid-

ed they would do. If the poacher did come, maybe he'd
be too busy laughing at me to harm me.

I always pray before going to bed, and this time I
really prayed. It's amazing how easy it is to talk to God
when your life's on the line. Staring at the ceiling, I
asked for the Lord's protection, not just for me but for
Felix and Sam too.

I looked at the clock: 11 P.M. Not good. If I didn't
get to sleep soon, getting up for church would be nearly impossible.

I could go downstairs for a glass of warm milk, but
my older sister, Amanda, was saying goodnight to her
boyfriend, Cameron. Between her perfume and his
cologne, I feared for my eyes, not to mention the ozone
layer. Amanda was 18 and had strawberry blonde hair.
My friends at school said she looked like a super
model. To keep her ego from soaring too high, I did my
part to pester her on a daily basis—for her own good,
of course.

Rolling over, I forced my eyes to stay shut. I recit-
ed Bible verses. I prayed some more. Then the wind
kicked up. I opened my eyes to the sight of branches
scratching at my window. They looked like claws out
to get me. Then Sadie, our cocker spaniel, started barking. Now what?

Moving to the window, I yelled for her to quiet
down, but she wouldn't. Sadie barked like crazy at
something behind our garage. I immediately thought of
raccoons because we had problems with them digging

in our trash. Grabbing my flashlight, I headed downstairs to scare them off.

Outside the night air felt like a frozen mist around my body. My legs shivered. My hands shook. Why was I so nervous? It felt like my heart would beat through my chest. I gripped the flashlight like a club, ready for anything. Sadie kept barking. I searched along the ground with the flashlight's beam.

Clang! Something bumped the trash can. Grabbing a stick with my free hand, I eased ahead toward the corner of the garage.

"Arghh!" I yelled, hoping to scare the raccoon away. My flashlight lit up the trash cans. Nothing moved. I examined the ground beneath the trash cans. No raccoon prints. Just boot prints in the soft ground. They looked fresh. But so did the trash. The prints could have been my dad's. Or Orville's. When Sadie saw me, she quit barking and gave me a peculiar look.

Extending my hand, I tried to pet her, but she bolted away toward the back of the yard. She barked louder than before. She was chasing something through the bushes. I joined the pursuit and caught sight of something. But what? A man with dark clothes? A moon shadow? I ran forward, aiming the flashlight at the branches. Where is it? *What* is it? I kept looking, but nothing appeared.

Finally, I headed back inside and up the stairs to my room.

"Willie, what were you doing outside?" my mom asked from her bedroom.

"Nothing, Mom. Sadie scared up some raccoons again," I replied.

"Oh. Goodnight, dear," she said.

As I climbed into bed, my heart was still pumping like a piston. I knew sleep wouldn't come easily. And I was right. I tossed and twisted, adjusted my pillow, and pulled up my covers. All I could think about was getting the tape to the game warden before the poacher got to me.

I must have finally dozed off because the next thing I knew, daylight was filtering through my window. I checked the clock: 8 A.M. Oh, no! I jumped out of bed. I had overslept. If I didn't fly, I'd never make it to church. Dashing down the stairs, I ran past the family room to the kitchen. I reached the table just before my mom removed the pancakes.

After filling my plate and pouring on the syrup, I gulped down my breakfast under the glares of my parents. *Hurry, eat,* I told myself. Soon a queasiness filled my stomach. Something wasn't right.

I looked up, perplexed. Maybe I was eating too fast or feeling guilty about being so late to breakfast. No, that wasn't it.

"Something's missing," I announced.

"It's Amanda and Orville," Dad said. "They've finished already."

"That's not it," I said. I thought for a moment. I had passed the family room and … Oh no! The video camera. I didn't remember seeing it. Jumping up from the table, I ran into the family room. I skidded to a stop.

The camera was gone.

A Whiff of Toxic Waste

It wasn't a dream. The man by the trash cans must have returned and stolen the tape after I fell asleep.

"Mom! Dad!" I yelled.

"What?" Dad asked, hurrying into the family room.

I pointed at the TV stand. "The camera's gone! Someone broke in last night and took it."

My dad grabbed my shoulders and fell to his knees. "Say it isn't so, Willie!" he begged, shaking me back and forth. "Say it isn't so."

I stared at my dad, not knowing if I should help him up or call the guys in the white coats to take him away. He was taking this a little too hard.

Then he let out a big laugh and stood up. "Relax, Willie. Phoebe's dad picked up the camera last night after you went to bed," my dad explained.

I dropped my shoulders in relief. Then a new fear hit me. What if Phoebe recorded over the scene with the poacher's net! I sprinted from the room and across the yard. In seconds I was pounding on her front door. It opened to Phoebe and her camera filming me.

"Here he is, the great Willie Plummet," she announced, "pajamas and all. Can you say 'Pooh Bear'?"

I grabbed the camera from Phoebe as quickly as I could, grumbling at my grandma for buying the pajamas and at myself for actually wearing them. "Phoebe, what'd you do with our tape?"

"Calm down," she said. "It's still in there."

I slapped my forehead. We had rewound the tape to where the net appeared.

"Phoebe," I asked, my voice quaking, "you didn't record over our footage, did you?"

She gave me a surprised look. "How dumb do you think I am? Of course not."

"You're the best, Phoebe." I breathed a sigh of relief. "Do you have any other tapes to record with?"

"I think so."

"Then do you mind if I hold onto this one for safe-keeping?"

"What for?"

"I'll explain later," I told her. With Phoebe's permission, I ejected the tape.

She quickly retrieved the camera. "Sorry, but this stays with me. I need it for church."

"What for?"

"I need to get some footage of you. You have nursery duty today. I checked the schedule."

I plugged my nose, realizing she was right. A month ago our youth pastor had challenged us junior highers to find ways to serve at church. The next thing I knew, I had signed up for a year of crying babies and dirty diapers.

"Film me today?" I pictured myself covered with spit up, a screaming Putz twin under each arm. "Who'd you say this video is for again?"

"My school," she answered matter-of-factly.

I lifted my eyebrows. "You mean your class?"

"No, my school. There's going to be an assembly next Monday, after we get back from our week off for teachers' conference. The whole school will be there, plus parents, brothers and sisters, everyone."

"Everyone?" I moaned.

Phoebe went to Washington Elementary—my old school. My former teachers would *love* her video. Watching my most embarrassing moments would be their way to get even for all the trouble I had caused—by accident, of course.

One time I had made a chocolate volcano for an assembly. Unfortunately the eruption exceeded my expectations and spewed chocolate all over the auditorium. After that, the only time I saw my teachers really happy was on my final day of sixth grade.

Not wanting to hear any more, I headed for home. I didn't know whom to fear more—Scrub and his death truck or Phoebe and her video camera. Good thing it was Sunday. With so much on my mind, I needed a little help from above.

Did I say a *little help* from above? I needed *a lot* of help. As in tons. God could send a legion of angels and I'd still be short-handed.

"Quiet, little tykes," I pleaded, ready to scream even louder than the dozen babies around me. Bubba Putz wailed in my ear. He had greeted the world at 10 pounds, 9 ounces and now weighed double that and then some. From the moment his parents dropped him off, Bubba had stopped crying only once, and that was to spit up on my shoulder.

In my other arm I held Morris, Bubba's twin brother. He was famous for dirtying his diapers to colossal proportions. And he was in no mood to disappoint me.

Felix noticed my face turning green. "Gives a whole new meaning to the phrase 'toxic waste,' doesn't it," he said, laughing.

"No wonder people are so opposed to chemical warfare," I replied and gasped for fresh air. I searched the room for earmuffs and a gas mask, convinced they should be standard issue for the nursery.

"Let's try singing," Felix suggested. He had a screaming baby in each arm and one in a crib that he was rocking with his foot.

I sing like a wounded cat, but I was desperate enough to try anything. "Jesus loves me, this …"

"They're screaming louder. Let's try a more up-tempo song," Felix begged.

We started the Noah's ark song. I imitated the sound of each animal Noah brought onto the ark. I barked like a dog, oinked like a pig, even quacked and waddled like a duck.

"This has to be the stupidest thing I have ever done," I said, looking out the windows for any sign of Phoebe and her video camera.

"Who cares! Phoebe's not around. Besides, it's working," Felix said. "More animals! Quick."

But I couldn't think of any and had to improvise with the one thing most on my mind. I became the Video Sub, cruising first this way, then that way, under the floating ark.

"Are you nuts?" Felix shouted above the screaming babies. "They want animals, not surveillance equipment."

He was right. The crying and screaming reached a dangerous pitch. Quickly we moved all the babies to the center of the room for fear the windows would shatter.

"Try a chicken," Felix suggested.

Time to go for broke, I decided. I put down the Putz twins and found a rubber glove to stretch over the top of my head. The empty fingers flopped back and forth when I nodded my head. "Do I look like a chicken?" I asked Felix.

"More like a dweeb," he said truthfully. "But at least you're a funny dweeb."

As Felix started the song again, I crouched down. "*Brawk, brawk, brawk.*" I fluttered my arms like wings and pecked at the floor. The rubber fingers from the glove flapped against my forehead. "*Brawk, brawk, brawk.*"

Suddenly, a burst of laughter came from the storage cabinet in the corner of the room. I recognized the voice, that high-pitched, girlish giggle.

"No!" I wailed. "Not again!"

The door swung open and out stepped Phoebe with her video camera. The red light above the lens blinked in my eyes like a beacon of doom.

"Bravo!" Phoebe laughed. "You were stupendous. The world's greatest chicken impression. Or the world's worst chicken impression. Who knows? The main thing is I caught it all on videotape. I can't wait to hear what people say about this."

If it weren't for the babies, I would have taken Phoebe's camera and cracked it open like an egg. "Give me that tape," I ordered.

"Forget it," she said. "Do you want my help with these babies or not?"

I didn't have to think for long. The answer screamed at me from every corner of the room. "Fine. Help us now and give me the tape later."

Phoebe grabbed two babies and bounced them up and down. She also sang sweetly. Even that wasn't enough. I looked at Felix. His head was bowed and his eyes were closed. I prayed that he was praying for a miracle. He must have been. Seconds later, in walked Sam.

"You guys," she said, "they can hear you in church!"

"Give us a break," I responded. "What else can we do?"

Sam appraised the situation. "These babies need something that will take their minds off how miserable they are in your care. They need some kind of treat."

"Willie and I sang for them," Felix told her.

Sam winced. "I said *treat*, not torture."

"Be our guest," I said.

Sam grabbed two brooms from the storage closet along with pink and blue baby blankets. In seconds she had tied up two flags and begun to twirl. She spun them around, snapped them up and down, and flipped them in the air.

"Amazing!" Phoebe said.

"That's for sure," Felix agreed. "Talk about practice paying off." One by one the babies stopped crying and began to watch, looking just as impressed as Phoebe and Felix and me.

That afternoon, Felix and Sam biked to my house. They listened as I called the game warden. He agreed to

look at the video and suggested we meet at Lunker Lake
so we could show him where the net was.

After another nerve-wracking ride, we found ourselves standing on the shore of the lake. The afternoon
sun burned like a hot iron on our shoulders. The glare
off the water made us squint. We wondered if the game
warden would make it. Then his green truck pulled up.
Behind the cab's rear window, a tool storage bin covered
part of the bed. The game warden waved us over without getting out of his truck.

"Do you have the tape?" he asked, looking around.
He definitely looked like a game warden with his neatly
trimmed hair and close shave. It was nice to come to
Lunker Lake and see an adult's face I could trust.

"Right here," I said, handing it over.

He eyed the tape. "This is the *only* copy?"

I nodded.

"Good," he said. "If the poacher saw this it could
ruin my investigation. He might even come looking for
you."

"Come looking for us?" Sam asked, her face full of
worry.

The warden stared at us. "You saw what happened
to the fish. If I were you, I'd forget about that net. Leave
the detective work to me."

"Net?" Felix asked. "What net? I never saw any net."

The game warden offered a reassuring smile.
"There you go."

We were about to explain where we had found the net when a truck engine echoed faintly across the water. It came from the direction of the bait shack. "There's your poacher," I told the warden.

"What are you talking about?" he asked. I explained what had happened with Scrub and my suspicion that he had been trying to run us down.

Before I finished, the game warden started his truck and pulled away from us. Water dripped from the bed. Pine needles flew in all directions—including ours. I ducked behind a tree, then chanced a peek as the green truck headed in the direction of the bait shack.

"Now what?" Felix asked.

"We can run over there and see what happens," Sam suggested.

"I think we should stay here," I said, "in case the game warden comes back. We never showed him where the net was. The videotape won't tell him where to look."

"Good point," Felix said, looking toward the bait shack. It was quiet there now, and both trucks had disappeared.

When two days had passed and we still hadn't heard anything, I decided to call the game warden for an update. The office clerk who answered said he was out sick and had been since Sunday.

"What about the poacher?" I asked. "Did you catch him?"

"The who?" the clerk asked.

"I gave the game warden a video that proves there's someone illegally netting fish in Lunker Lake," I explained.

"It sounds like you'll need to speak with the game warden," the clerk replied, totally uninterested.

"Will he be in tomorrow?" I asked.

"I doubt it. But if you want to leave your name and number, I'll see that he gets it."

"Do you know what's wrong with him?" I asked.

"No, I'm afraid not," the clerk said. "No one in the office does."

I gave her the information then hung up, afraid that something had gone wrong. Surely the game warden would tell his co-workers about a poacher—especially if he was going to be out sick.

After a quick conference call to Felix and Sam, we agreed to return to Lunker Lake with the Video Sub and have a look around. Sam was just as suspicious as I was. Felix thought it was out of our hands but came along to operate the Video Sub.

Retracing our steps, we made our way along Lunker Lake. With the blue sky overhead, ripples shimmering on the water, and birds singing all around, it was hard to imagine the fish harvest going on below the surface. But we knew it was true.

We launched the Video Sub and held our breath as the submarine approached the spot where we'd found the net. With my eyes glued to the sonar screen, I prepared for the blinking dot to stop.

"Anything?" Felix asked.

"We're not there yet," Sam told him. "It's right up here." We stepped forward carefully.

"Just a few more feet," Sam said. "Three. Two. One. Now!"

We stopped in our tracks and stared at the screen, convinced the sub would stop with us. But it didn't. The light blinked and moved ahead.

Felix whacked the sonar screen, then searched across the water, baffled. But Lunker Lake offered no clues. He turned the Video Sub around and brought it back across the net's previous location. It didn't even slow down.

I shook my head. "There goes our proof."

"What did you expect?" Sam argued. "Someone came to your house to steal the videotape. When that didn't work, he removed the net. End of the evidence. End of the story."

"Maybe," Felix said, his eyes brightening, "or maybe he moved the net to a better spot." Felix turned the Video Sub and we hiked along a new section of shoreline.

Sam continued to log the time as the submarine passed key markers. Felix operated the remote control. I watched the sonar screen while praying for an answer. After walking to the bend at the far end of Lunker Lake, we retrieved the submarine.

"Now what?" Sam asked, voicing the frustration we all felt.

"Let's leave," I said. Turning around, I searched the trees as if a clue would suddenly appear. Nothing did. We loaded up the Video Sub and our gear and headed for home.

The first thing we did when we walked in the house was connect the camera to my TV. Then we sat down to watch the new footage, hoping to see some remnant of the poacher's work. But no evidence appeared. Plenty of mud and minnows and weeds drifted by, but no fishing nets of any kind.

What a letdown. We had given the one tape we had to the warden and he was missing. First, some poacher cleaned out all the fish in Lunker Lake. Then, he got rid of his illegal net. "Why wouldn't the game warden have told his secretary about the poacher?" I asked, frustrated up to my eyeballs and venting to no one in particular.

"Maybe he doesn't trust her," Felix reasoned. "If the poacher has a contact on the inside, he'll always be one step ahead of the law."

"But why wouldn't the warden tell us?" Sam asked.

Then it hit me. "Maybe he can't. Maybe instead of getting the poacher, the poacher got him." An eerie silence settled over us as we thought about the possibility.

Suddenly, it made sense to me. "Now that I think about it, the clerk didn't say the game warden *called in* sick, she said he was *out* sick. Maybe she was covering up what really happened."

"You could be right," Felix admitted. "But either way the question is *what now*?"

Sam jumped right in. "That's easy. Where did we see the game warden last?"

"Peeling out for the bait shack," Felix answered.

"Then that's where we go," Sam stated. "I've heard enough about this Scrub. I'd like to see him for myself."

The next day Sam wanted us to stop by her house before we rode our bikes to the bait shack. We found her in the sewing room with her mom. She was trying on her outfit for the fall invitational. The top was purple. The skirt was gold with shimmering sparkles.

"Almost done," Mrs. Stewart said as she pinned the hem on the skirt. "There. The length looks just right. Now if we can check the other two, you kids can be on your way."

"How long will that take?" I moaned, eager to get going. I pictured Felix and myself covered with cobwebs as Sam tried on outfit after outfit.

"That's up to you and Felix," Sam replied, revealing a peculiar grin.

I didn't know what she had in mind, but I knew I didn't like it. "What do you mean, 'up to us'?"

"My mom made the skirts for the entire flag team. Everyone has come by to try theirs on except two girls. We need you and Felix to …"

"No way. Not even. Won't happen," I interrupted. I looked around suspiciously and even opened the closet door. "This has Phoebe written all over it. Where is she?"

"Phoebe's not here. I promise," Sam said. "Besides, the girls who haven't shown up are the same height as you two, otherwise I would try them on myself. Hurry up. My mom wants to get the lengths right before we leave."

Felix backed toward the door. "I'm with Willie on this one. Sorry, Sam."

"You guys! Come on. You can slide them on over your jeans. It will take two minutes, max." She pushed a skirt at me. "Willie, it would be helpful *and* admirable."

I pushed it back. "You're dreaming."

"So this is the thanks I get?" Sam shook her head and tossed the skirt down. "The babies at church were screaming their heads off, burning holes in their diapers, and turning you into barn animals. Then I arrived and saved the day. But now that I ask you for one small favor …"

"Okay. Okay. We'll do it." Felix said, grabbing a skirt.

"What do you mean *we*?" I objected.

"It's no big deal," Felix argued. "Besides, Phoebe's not around. Quit being so paranoid."

I checked the closet again, then looked down the hall. Next I rummaged through the drawers beneath the sewing machine.

"Phoebe's not *that* small," Sam told me.

"No, but she's crafty. And she's made a career of spying on me." I looked around the room. There were piles of clothes and boxes that I could inspect, but I decided not to. Maybe I *was* being paranoid. Still, just to be safe, I closed the door to the sewing room and locked it. "Fine, but make it fast."

We slipped the skirts on over our jeans and stood next to Sam so her mom could compare the lengths.

"Looks good," Mrs. Stewart said. "Now step from side to side so I can see how they move."

"Felix," I asked, "do you feel as stupid as you look?"

"No, but I feel as stupid as you look," he replied.

I'm not sure who came out ahead on that exchange, so I changed the subject. "Are we done yet?"

"Almost," Sam answered. "There's just one more thing. My mom needs to check the length when you're doing the splits. Go ahead and ..."

I waved my hands in defiance. "That's it! I'm outta here."

Sam busted up right away. So did her mom.

"She's joking, Willie," Mrs. Stewart said. "We're done."

As fast as I have ever taken anything off, I got out of that skirt. So did Felix. We waited in the kitchen while Sam changed. I drank a glass of cold water, trying to cool down. That's when I saw Phoebe. She strolled up the driveway and walked in the front door, her camera case slung over her shoulder.

"Too late," I said, letting out a laugh. "You missed your chance to embarrass me big time. This would have been the gold medal of all embarrassments. Not only was I doing something admirable, but I was wearing something no guy would ever be caught dead wearing. And you missed it. Hah, Hah. Nice try. You snooze, you loose." I danced around Phoebe like I was the heavyweight champion of the world. It felt so good to have finally outfoxed her.

"Really?" Phoebe asked, showing no regret. She pressed her lips together as if trying to contain herself. She walked straight for the sewing room. I quit laughing and followed.

Phoebe stepped into the room, glanced at the skirts that Sam's mom was hemming, then reached into a pile of material next to the sewing machine. "There you are," Phoebe said. She removed the video camera with its blinking red light. "Look, I accidentally left the record button on. What a waste of film. I'm sure *nothing* good happened in here."

Sam, Mrs. Stewart, and Phoebe exchanged looks, then doubled over laughing. Felix and I just stood there, stunned, while they cracked up. Soon they were passing tissues to dab their watering eyes.

"This time I'm *really* outta here," I told Felix, knowing Sam was still too hysterical to hear a word I said.

When we pushed through the bait shack door, Scrub jumped. Then he stared us down as if we had done something wrong. His gray hair frizzed on his head like he was drowning in static. "Look who's back," he muttered, his Tootsie Roll eyebrow weighing heavily on his forehead.

"Just wondering what they're biting on," I said, trying to remain calm.

"They're not," he growled. "There's not a bait on the planet that will catch fish in this miserable lake."

"Why not?" Sam asked.

Scrub tightened his jaw. " 'Cause there aren't any fish to catch."

"I guess there's always Pinnacle Lake," Felix offered.

"No, there isn't," Scrub countered. "Not anymore. You'll catch more fish here than there."

"What are you talking about?" I protested. "The other day you said the action was great up there."

"It was. But now the fishing's dead. Take my advice: Stay away from Pinnacle Lake."

Here we go again, I thought. I remembered the first time Scrub had given me that warning. It had been about Lunker Lake when it hid an illegal net. Was he trying to keep us away from Pinnacle Lake for the same reason?

"Where should we try then?" Sam asked.

"Beats me," Scrub said. "If you're that hungry for fish, go to the market. There's nothing to catch in these parts."

Time to push ahead, I decided. "Maybe we should check with the game warden," I suggested, watching for Scrub's reaction. "I bet he knows where the fish are."

Scrub jerked his coffee cup, spilling some on his magazine. "The game warden?" he said, a sneer crossing his face. "Sure. Try him. See what he has to say about catching fish."

I stepped closer. "We can't find him. You don't know where he is, do you?"

Scrub looked around nervously, then picked up a paper towel to clean the spill. He tried to look uninterested in our conversation, but I could tell something was bugging him. "Sorry. Can't say as I do."

"You're sure?" I argued.

"Yep."

Not satisfied, I meandered to the back of the store. I milled around, listening for muffled cries for help. I pictured the game warden on the floor of a storage room, tied and gagged.

Scrub watched me over the top of his magazine every step of the way. "Can I help you find something?"

"Just looking," I said. There was a door just a few feet away. It had to lead to a small storage area. If the game warden were unconscious, there'd be no cries for help. I had to check behind that door.

"Let's go, Willie," Sam said. She and Felix moved toward the front door.

I looked at the storage room door again. Scrub wasn't looking. It had to be now, but I needed an alibi.

Then I remembered Scrub's wisecrack from a few days ago. Perfect.

"I need to use the rest room," I said. "Give me a minute."

I grabbed the doorknob and flung open the storage room door. Darkness blinded me.

"Hey, what are you doing?" Scrub demanded. He charged toward me, his heavy boots banging like thunder on the wood floor.

I needed light—now! But I couldn't find the light switch. My hand groped spastically up and down the wall. I moved ahead before Scrub could catch me. My eyes began to adjust to the gloom. A mop and bucket rested in one corner. Boxes of fishing gear lined some shelves along with soda cans and food, but there was no game warden. Then I saw a door at the back of the storage room. A heavy *thud* came from the other side, then another *bump* echoed through the door. Someone was in there.

Scrub filled the doorway to the storage room, blocking the light. "Get away from there," he ordered.

I had to save the warden. I grabbed the doorknob.

"Get back," Scrub demanded.

I took a deep breath and swung the door open.

Big mistake. I mean *BIG MISTAKE*!

8

Scrub's Secret

A giant alligator snapped his jaws right at me! His eyes burned. His teeth dripped. His tail thumped against the wall.

I stared in horror. I couldn't move or speak. The alligator slithered toward my legs.

"Get back!" Scrub yelled. He yanked my arm and stood between me and the alligator. "You want to get yourself killed?"

"N-n-no," I whimpered, still in shock.

Scrub grabbed a fish from a barrel and tossed it to the alligator. The monster's powerful jaws chomped it in two, then gulped down both pieces.

"That could have been your leg," Scrub said, glaring at me.

After backing me out of the way, Scrub closed the door and pushed me into the store. "Next time, listen to me when I tell you to get back."

Felix hurried over. "What happened in there?"

Sam eyed me closely. "Willie, is your hair getting redder?"

"Nope, it's his face," Felix said. "It's whiter."

"What's so scary about a storeroom?" Sam asked, looking warily at Scrub.

Scrub shrugged as if he was clueless. "Beats me."

That did it. "Al-al-alligator!" I stammered, grabbing their collars. "He has an alligator! And it almost ate me for lunch."

"Whose fault is that?" Scrub asked. "Molly was just defending her space like any dog would do."

"Dogs play catch and lick your face," I said, still shaking.

Scrub grabbed my arm. "I can have Molly lick your face if you want."

"That's all right," I said. Squirming loose from his thick hand, I headed for the door. Felix and Sam followed right behind. Outside, I paused a moment to calm down. Adrenaline pumped through my body like a geyser. My skin felt damp and hot at the same time.

"Let's get out of here," Sam said. She grabbed her bike and mine and walked them. She could tell I was in no shape to ride. I followed behind, my body still tingling. Sam and Felix paused by Scrub's truck.

"Talk about big tires," Felix said. "Hey, Willie, imagine those treads imprinted on your face."

Sam joined in. "Beats having Molly lick it. Right, Willie?"

"Does it?" I asked, not too happy with either option. "Why does the endangered face have to belong to me? You both have faces."

"But yours is so cute," Sam said, squeezing my cheek.

I didn't know if I should gag or blush. I changed the subject. "Too bad we don't have Phoebe's video camera. I'd like to get these tracks on video."

"What for?" Felix asked.

"All I hear is trucks—at the lake, in the woods, by my house. I'd like to know which is which," I explained.

"Say no more," Sam exclaimed. She removed the video camera from her bike bag. "Phoebe said we could borrow it. I guess the footage she got of you in the flag team uniform made her real happy."

"Is that tape still in there?" I asked, thinking I could erase the whole thing.

"Are you nuts? She would never let *that* go," Sam said with a chuckle.

We moved to a spot out of eyesight from the bait shack window. Sam hit the record button on the camera. Carrying it like a football, she jogged back to Scrub's truck. She filmed the tires and the tracks beneath them.

As soon as Sam returned, we loaded up our bikes and took off as fast as we could. On the way home I tried to make the best of the situation. "At least now if a truck runs us down, we can compare the tread on our faces to Scrub's tires."

"You're the man, Willie," Sam replied, no doubt impressed with my logic.

But Felix wasn't satisfied with just comparing truck tires. "This whole thing stinks," he finally said. "Thanks to that alligator we don't know *who* planted that net or *why*."

"What are you talking about?" I asked.

"We only *think* Scrub did it. Maybe the game warden planted the net to catch the alligator," Felix offered.

"Why would he wipe out a lake's entire population of trout and bass to catch one alligator?" Sam asked.

"The alligator would kill the fish anyway," Felix reasoned. "Not to mention any swimmers who showed up."

"I don't buy it," I responded. "I still think Scrub's the poacher. The alligator guards the net and gets a few fish in return. Who needs a guard dog when you've got a guard gator? Scrub sells the rest of the fish he catches for profit."

Felix shook his head. "But he sells bait for a living. Why would he wipe out the fish and ruin his own business?"

I stopped my bike, confident that I had figured the whole thing out. "You tell me what pays more: selling worms to fishermen or selling trout to restaurants. Once the fish are gone, the Fish and Wildlife Department plants thousands more. Six months from now Scrub does the same thing all over again."

"But why would he use an alligator to guard the traps?" Sam asked.

"Can you think of a better way to get rid of pesky game wardens?" I asked, staring at Felix and Sam. "Or kids?"

The thought of becoming alligator chow left me feeling a little edgy. The rest of the way to Glenfield I freaked out over every little sound. "What was that?" I asked.

"A bird," Sam told me. "It chirped. That's what birds do. They chirp."

"It didn't sound like a bird," I replied.

"Maybe it's carrying a video camera," Felix put in, "to get a shot of the alligator eating you for a snack."

"What?" I choked, searching the sky.

"Relax, Willie," Sam said. "He was joking."

Sam was right. I needed to relax. If only it were that easy.

We stopped in the front yard of my house. Felix and Sam had to get home, but I wanted to agree on our next move before they left.

"Pinnacle Lake," I told them. "We have to go there, it makes perfect sense."

Felix kicked the ground. "I was afraid you'd say that."

"It's the only way to know for sure. Felix, if your theory is right and the game warden set the net to catch the alligator, he won't take the net to Pinnacle Lake," I explained. "But if *I'm* right, Scrub's net is already up there. That's why he's telling everyone to stay away."

"When do you want to go?" Sam asked.

"Tomorrow, first thing, before Scrub hauls all the fish out and hides his net," I said.

Sam shook her head. "I can't go. I have the fall invitational. Besides, Pinnacle Lake is surrounded by cliffs and brush. There's no way to walk around it."

"In that case we can forget it," Felix said, looking relieved.

But I wouldn't give up. "So we borrow a boat and go after Sam's finished."

Sam laughed. "Even if we could find a boat, are you going to pull it behind your bike?"

"I'll talk to Orville," I said, starting to feel irritated. "He can take us in his truck."

Sam looked doubtful. "If we're not walking the shore, how will we monitor our location in the logbook? Ripples on the water don't make a very permanent landmark."

"I know I'm going to regret this later," Felix said, letting out a big sigh, "but we may not need the logbook."

"What do you mean?" I asked.

Felix grinned. "Let's just say I've been doing a little thinking."

9

Willie's Worst Nightmare

I hung up the phone. Rejection number 14. What a disaster. Just two hours since we agreed to try Pinnacle Lake and it was looking bleak. It's not that I didn't know any boat owners. They just wouldn't loan their precious vessels to a bunch of kids.

"But what if Orville goes?" I kept asking, my voice pleading. "He always tells me that he's a *man among men.*"

At that everyone started to laugh, which is pretty much how I had reacted when Orville first said it to me. I tried changing my technique, but that didn't help either. By the time the day was over, I still didn't have a boat.

I climbed the stairs to my bedroom and collapsed on my bed. *Lord, what's going on here?* I asked, still determined to solve the mystery of Lunker Lake. Dad and I had talked about it at dinner. He thought we should quit worrying about it and find something else to do. Something productive. Hearing about the alligator made him even more convinced that the Fish and Wildlife Department had set the net.

"It was obviously to catch the alligator," he had told me during dinner. "That's why the net is gone now."

"Then why didn't the game warden get rid of the alligator instead of leaving it at the bait shack?" I questioned.

"The game warden's sick—give the guy a break," Orville blurted out, broccoli bits spewing from his mouth. "Once he's well the alligator will be transported to a zoo someplace."

But I still didn't buy it. The more I thought about it and reconstructed the mysterious events, the more freaked out I got. First, a giant death truck almost ground us into roadkill. Second, the poacher prowled around my house, trying to steal the tape. Third, as soon as the game warden got a look at the tape, he disappeared. And fourth, an alligator nearly ate me alive just for going into the wrong room. *No, something's definitely wrong*, I told myself. *Definitely wrong.*

I rolled over in bed, determined to solve the mystery. But my eyelids kept getting heavier, like lead fishing weights were pulling them down. *Help me figure this out, Lord*, I prayed as my eyes closed. *After all, we are dealing with Your creation.*

Brrrnnng, brrnng. I sat up, ready to clobber Orville for setting my alarm clock. I'd only been in bed a few minutes.

"Willie? Phone for you," my mom's muffled voice rose in the stairwell.

Stumbling to my parents' bedroom, I picked up the phone. Felix greeted me with, "It's not looking good, Willie."

"So what else is new?" I replied.

He explained that the submarine transmitter wouldn't send a video signal. "Radio waves are a cinch, but that's as much as I've figured out."

This isn't happening, I told myself. Nothing was going right. "Just keep trying, Felix," I finally managed to tell him. With that I dragged myself back to bed.

Like the first night of our misadventure, sleep didn't come easily. I yanked and kicked at my sheets until they came untucked. When Amanda got home, I thought about closing the door to my bedroom. Her boyfriend was staying to watch TV and I feared that the fumes from their perfume-cologne cloud would kill me in my sleep. But I stayed in bed.

Eventually the TV went silent. The lights in the rest of the house went out. The voices stopped. It was quiet and dark—time to slumber deeply. But my eyelids wouldn't cooperate. They would snap open as soon as I shut them. At first I fought back, squeezing my eyelids shut. Then I wondered if God wasn't keeping me awake for a reason.

I strained to listen, my ears perked. I feared Scrub would make another visit to our house. Maybe he had seen us videotape his tires and was afraid we had dis-covered some crucial evidence. Maybe he would come for the tape … or for me. I lifted my head from the pillow, straining to listen. I expected a truck's engine to shatter the quiet night at any moment.

But that's not what I heard. A heavy thump came from the bottom of the stairs. Then another. Two more followed. It sounded like two people walking in stride, only slightly off. It sounded like bare feet with toenails long enough to scratch the floor.

Th-thump. Th-thump.

Whatever it was, it was climbing the stairs toward my room. I stared at the door. It was open! Why hadn't I closed it before going to sleep? Of all the nights to leave it open!

Th-thump. Th-thump.

The noise neared the top of the stairs. I pulled my covers to my chin. The creature grumbled from deep in its throat. If I could just close the door—but I couldn't move. I couldn't yell. I shook in horror.

Th-thump. Th-thump. Grrrrr.

The alligator filled my doorway. Molly the Mutilator. Her jaws opened, teeth dripping saliva.

"No!" I screamed. But my "scream" was as quiet as a whisper.

The alligator darted into my room, heading straight for me. I squirmed to the corner of my bed. I curled up under the covers. Molly's teeth snapped into the blanket. I felt a tug. But I wouldn't let go. I gripped the blanket tighter, like a lifeline.

Grrrrr. The alligator pulled harder, snapping her head back and forth.

"No! No!" I screamed.

"Yes, yes!" the alligator responded in a human girl-ish voice. "Willie, get up already."

I loosened my grip, confused. When did the alligator learn my name? Or learn how to speak, for that matter. With a final *grrrrr*, the blanket pulled free. I opened my eyes.

Phoebe stood over me. Sadie held the blanket in her teeth.

"It was only a nightmare," I said, too freaked out to move. Then I saw the video camera in my face and realized the nightmare wasn't over.

"Not again, Phoebe." I tried to get my blanket back so I could hide under it, but Sadie dragged it across the room.

Phoebe narrated as she filmed. "Here he is, the legendary Willie Plummet, back from Oogie-Boogie Land. Have a nice trip, Wilbur, my dear?"

"Don't ask," I said, rubbing the sleep from my eyes.

"That's all right, Willie. Your loyal fans still believe in you." Phoebe zoomed in. "Even though you did wet your bed."

"What?" I jumped up and felt the mattress.

Phoebe burst out laughing while recording my every move. "I'm kidding. You *are* jumpy, aren't you. What's wrong?"

I filled her in on my alligator episode, along with a detailed explanation of the events that had led up to it. Phoebe listened intently to the whole thing. It's not hard to feel like a big shot when you hear "That's awesome!" "You're amazing!" or "That's so cool!" after every statement.

"Phoebe, you're all right," I told her, realizing that a little video admiration wasn't such a bad thing after all. She was always there to make me feel like a hero.

I stared at the camera with a new sense of determination. "It's not just about poachers or fishing nets or alligators. It's about truth, and today, I, Wilbur Plummet, great-great-grandson of the legendary Jedediah Plummet, will find it." Jedediah Plummet had been a pioneer of aviation. In fact, it was by studying his designs that the Wright Brothers had learned what *not* to do if they wanted to fly.

Phoebe shut off the camera. "That was incredible, Willie."

"Thanks. Now do you mind leaving me alone so I can get dressed?"

"*Excuse me*, Mr. Hotshot Save-the-World Celebrity." Phoebe turned up her nose and left the room. Sadie followed along.

Sitting on my bed, I paused to say another little prayer, knowing that without the Lord's help I could never solve the mystery of Lunker Lake.

10

So Long Tape Delay

Enough's enough, I thought. I would have to wake Orville up. Orville is a typical high school student. He loves to sleep in. And since it was still vacation for teachers' conference, he was in his glory. But I needed his help, and I couldn't wait any longer.

Pushing open Orville's door, I eased ahead. Maybe if I was gentle and didn't startle him, he wouldn't go psycho on me. Good thing Phoebe wasn't around with her camera. If she filmed this, the excessive violence might be too graphic for young viewers.

"Orville, buddy?" I said softly. He didn't respond. Not good for me. He was really out, as in, "Don't even think of waking me." But I had to.

"Orville," I repeated, nudging his arm. He gurgled, then turned over.

Really not good.

"Earth to Orville, *man among men.*" Maybe a compliment would cool his burning anger over being awakened. In my dreams. His hand shot forward and grabbed my throat.

"If it's before 10 A.M., you're dead," Orville grumbled with a groggy voice. He squinted at me with a bloodshot eye, then checked his clock radio. 10:07 A.M.

"Thank You, God," I choked, wondering how long my breath would hold out.

Orville relinquished his grip, then propped himself up on his elbow. "This better be good or you're still dead."

"What can I do for you today?" I asked.

Orville looked around, expecting a trick. He's the suspicious type. "What do you mean?"

"Name the chore. I'll take care of it," I promised, daring to sit on his bed.

"Sure you will," Orville replied, dropping his head on his pillow. "What do you want?"

"A small favor, that's all." Orville just looked at me. "Okay. I need a ride to Pinnacle Lake," I said.

"That's it?"

"Pretty much. We'll need to take Felix, Sam, and a boat too, but that's about it."

"A boat!" Orville cried. "Where did you find a boat?

"I haven't yet. But I will."

Orville thought for a moment. "If this messes up my truck …"

"It won't. I promise."

"In that case, sure. No problem."

That's it? Just like that? *Life's too good*, I thought. I headed for the door. "Thanks, Orville."

"Anytime," he replied. "As soon as you finish my work at the hobby store, we'll get going."

I stopped in my tracks. "Your *work*?"

"Inventory, vacuuming, washing the windows, counting the parts in the opened model battleship box to make sure they're all there, and whatever else Dad says. You should be done by this afternoon." Orville chuckled and fluffed up his pillow. "Close the door on your way out."

"I should have known," I said, shaking my head. "I should have known."

Orville's prediction wasn't too far off. At 1 P.M. I was finishing the windows in front of my dad's hobby shop. Everything else was done. Felix was in the lab trying to rig the Video Sub for a live viewing. He seemed to be making some progress. In fact, everything was looking good, except for one small problem. No boat. I had called everyone I knew. But still no boat.

I stood there, my squeegee dripping, drowning in my frustration. What a waste to have come so far only to stop with my mystery unsolved. As soon as I finished the window, I would go to the lab and tell Felix to call it off. Better to save the favor from Orville for future use than to waste it driving up to Pinnacle Lake just to stand on the shore. I made a final swipe with the squeegee, then collected the bucket and ladder.

"Looks good, Willie," Dad said, inspecting my work. "The phone's for you. It's Sam. She said something about a boat."

"A boat? As in she found one?" I asked.

My dad shrugged. "Beats me."

I hurried inside and grabbed the receiver. "Sam, what's this about a boat? I thought you were at the competition."

"I am. But we have long breaks between rounds. Now here's the good news. I talked to my coach about us needing a boat. Her friend, Steve Crubble, has a canoe we can borrow."

"You're serious?"

"Sure am," Sam announced. "Now aren't you glad I'm on the flag team?"

"I'm getting there," I said.

"Mr. Crubble won't be home until later, but his wife is expecting you and Orville after the competition," Sam continued.

"After? Why can't we go now?" I asked.

Sam cleared her throat like I had just said the wrong thing. "Because I'm in the finals and you and Felix are coming to see me perform. Right?"

"Oh yeah. Don't worry, we'll be there."

The fall invitational was held in the football stadium at Glenfield High School. It was only a short walk from Plummet's Hobbies. When we arrived, Sam's team was next to compete. Perfect timing—Felix and I could watch her, then finish getting ready for our trip to Pinnacle Lake. Felix needed to complete his modifications to the Video Sub. Orville and I had to pick up the canoe.

As soon as Sam's mom spotted us, she came right over. "Sam's team made it through the preliminary rounds. If they score high enough on their next routine, they will win it all."

I stared at the girls, feeling self-conscious. I didn't know whose skirt I had tried on, and I didn't want to know. Too bad I didn't mention that to Mrs. Stewart.

"The girl with the red hair," Mrs. Stewart said, pointing. "That's your skirt."

"Not so loud, please," I pleaded through clenched teeth, looking over my shoulder for Leonard "the Crusher" Grubb. "It's not *my* skirt anyway. I was just being admirable."

"I know," she said. "I'm just teasing you."

Fun for her, torture for me. Why had I put that thing on? I was still thinking about it when Sam's team snapped into action.

Music blasted over the giant loudspeakers. All the girls moved together, covering the field. Flags snapped through the air. Poles twirled about, up and down and around again. The motion flowed like honey, each girl in unison with the other.

"Not bad," Felix said, obviously impressed.

I was too. I felt bad for my wisecrack about flag team not being cool. Sam was good at this and she was having fun. So what if someone else didn't like it.

"Look at Sam's arms," Felix observed. "She flings that heavy pole around like it's a toothpick."

I patted Felix on the back. "I'm telling you, Sam should be your bodyguard, just in case Leonard Grubb sees that video of you wearing a skirt."

"If he sees me, he'll see you," Felix warned.

"Oh, yeah," I said, wishing I hadn't brought it up.

We watched in awe as the girls criss-crossed, ran backward, spun their flags first around their feet, then high in the air. Finally they lined up side by side, facing the audience. They raised their flags, then lowered them, like a giant wave moving from one end of the squad to the other. The second the music ended, they froze. The audience erupted with cheers and applause. Felix and I joined in, determined to cheer the loudest.

Soon the scores were announced. The crowd grew quiet. We waited, hoping.

"Yes!" I shouted, lifting my hands in the air. Sam's team had the highest score. First place was their's. Felix and I slapped high fives and jumped around.

Mrs. Stewart clapped wildly, her face radiant. I looked for Mr. Stewart, eager to see his reaction, but I couldn't find him. Then I remembered Sam's comment about her dad disapproving of flag team. Surely he wouldn't miss this, though. I moved through the crowd, thinking maybe he had stood somewhere else to get a better view. But I couldn't find him.

I turned toward the bleachers. Where was he? I scanned the audience. The faces blended together, nothing distinct. But wait! No. It couldn't be. The scruffy hair. The big long eyebrow. It was Scrub staring back at me. My mouth dropped open. I had to tell Felix. I worked my way back through the crowd.

"Felix, he's here, watching us!" I grabbed Felix and pointed toward the bleachers. But Scrub was gone.

Felix and I congratulated Sam without mentioning Scrub. Then I went home to find Orville so we could pick up the canoe.

Orville turned his truck down Crater Lane. "I can't believe I'm doing this," he moaned. "What are we looking for anyway?"

"It's at the end of the street," I explained. "Number 1072. It's a small one-story house with a gravel front yard."

"How nice. You're sure everything's set up?"

"Positive. Sam's coach got the okay earlier today."

"I still don't like it," Orville muttered. "We don't even know these people."

"We will soon," I said.

Orville pulled up in front of the house and I got out. A woman with gray hair and wrinkles around her eyes answered the door. "Mrs. Crubble?" I asked.

"Yes. You must be Wilbur," Mrs. Crubble said nervously. She wrung her hands on a dish towel that looked as old as her skin. She nodded toward the truck. "Who's that?"

"My brother, Orville."

"Well, why don't you have him pull around back. You can load the boat there."

I waved Orville around, then followed her through the house. A giant rainbow trout hung above the fireplace. "Now that's a trophy," I said, truly impressed.

"My husband caught that six years ago. He's quite the angler when he's not working. Lately he's working all the time, though. That's where he is now."

"It's sure nice of him to lend us his canoe," I said.

Mrs. Crubble smiled. "Now don't think too much of it. He has a fancy boat with all the bells and whistles. He leaves it in a dock so it's always ready. This one he just keeps around for emergencies."

I wanted to tell her that this was definitely an emergency but decided it would be better not to bring her in on the story. Besides, she looked uneasy enough as it was.

We went outside. Trees and flowers surrounded a huge pond in the backyard.

"Wow. Your husband is into fishing, isn't he!" I said. Orville pulled up and we loaded the canoe into his truck.

As we pulled away, Mrs. Crubble waved with the dish towel.

Our next stop was Sam's house. Then we returned to the hobby store. Felix was supposed to be waiting for us in the lab. I hoped the live video signal would be ready.

When Sam and I walked into the lab, it was empty—no Felix in sight. And someone had pulled the blinds on the back window. A creepy darkness filled the room.

"What's going on?" Sam asked suspiciously.

I couldn't blame it on Orville or my dad. Orville had walked up front to help Dad with a customer.

"Felix?" I asked, looking around. Then it hit me. The Video Sub. Was it gone too? I started to fear the worst. Had the poacher crept in and kidnapped Felix along with the submarine? I headed to the bathroom and flipped on the light. Still no Felix.

"Willie! Quick, come here." Sam's voice sounded urgent.

"What? What?" I said, returning to the lab.

"I found the Video Sub. It's over here." Sam stood near the back window. The submarine sat on a shelf above us.

"What's it doing up there?" I wondered out loud. "And where's Felix?" I studied the front window of the Video Sub. Everything looked fine, including Phoebe's camera. Not only that, everything looked the same too. "Oh, great," I muttered. "Felix the super scientist didn't change a thing."

"What'd you call me?" a voice asked.

I looked around, baffled. Sam joined me as we spun in circles, scanning the lab.

"Who said that?" I asked the empty space.

"Who do you think?" the voice replied. "By the way Willie, you have a piece of food in your teeth. I think it's spinach."

I jerked my head around, realizing that I recognized the voice."Felix, is that you?"

"The super scientist himself."

"Where are you? You better not have died and gone to heaven … at least not yet," I said, picking the spinach from my teeth. "We have a mystery to solve."

Felix laughed. "The mystery is me."

"Meaning what?" Sam asked. "You're the poacher?"

"No, but I've built you a submarine that can find him."

"The live video feed?" I asked. "You did it?

"I'm not in the room am I?" Felix countered.

Sam stared at the sub. "If you can see me live, tell me what I just did."

"Blew me a kiss," Felix replied. "I'm flattered. But if Willie does that I might get sick."

"Don't worry," I said. "Now where are you?"

"In the parking lot behind the store. You'll see a cable running out through the back window. Follow it to me." We found the cable where Felix said and followed it to Orville's truck. Felix sat in the front seat watching a small color TV and holding a walkie-talkie.

"Ta da!" Felix said as we arrived. On the screen we could see a shot of the lab just as we had left it. "Impressed?"

"Totally," Sam said. "But why didn't you think of this before? A cable doesn't seem that complicated."

"The key was the boat. As soon as Willie found one, I knew this would work. If we were on shore, the cable would snag in weeds along the bottom or in tree roots or branches. But as long as the Video Sub stays right below the boat, we won't have a problem."

"How could I have doubted you?" I asked.

"I was wondering the same thing," Felix replied. After turning off the TV monitor, he went inside to retrieve the Video Sub. He returned to the truck, carrying the sub and winding up the cable. We helped Felix load everything into the truck.

Sam, Felix, and I sat in the truck. Orville said he would be ready to take us in a few minutes. In the meantime we stared at our feet. A wave of nervous fear came over us. All the unbelievable events of the last week came down to this afternoon. So many questions filled my head. Would we find another net? Would the game warden turn up? What about Scrub?

Maybe nothing would happen at Pinnacle Lake, but I didn't think so. For some reason I had a feeling we would find far more than a few small fish and that the boat ride would be anything but boring.

11

Canoe Crashing

We knew that Felix tended to get carsick so Sam and I let him sit up front with Orville on the ride to Pinnacle Lake. But that didn't seem to be enough to help calm his stomach down. The turns were sharper and the hills steeper than on the road to Lunker Lake. Sam and I watched Felix closely from the cramped extended cab behind the front seat.

"Felix," I said, "your face looks kind of funny. Even more funny than normal."

"Sort of Kermit-the-Frog green," Sam added. Soon beads of sweat formed on Felix's face. We told him to roll down the window, fearful he'd loose his cookies at any moment.

"Just don't barf on me," I begged. I could see it now. The moment Felix used my shirt as a motion-sickness bag, the glove compartment would drop open. Out would crawl Phoebe with her video camera and miserable blinking red light.

"That's a little better," Felix said after sticking his face out the window.

"What happened to your glasses?" Orville asked. "You look like a human windshield." Splattered bugs covered each lens on Felix's glasses. He brought his face inside, gave us a dismal look, then put his face back outside. Needless to say, we all were relieved when Pinnacle Lake came into view.

"You made it," Sam said, patting Felix on the shoulder.

Felix wiped the sweat from his forehead. "Thank You, God." Orville parked the truck where the road ended, about 50 feet from the lake.

"Be back here in two hours," he said. After helping us unload the canoe, Orville drove off to fish a stream we had crossed a few miles back.

The three of us stared at Pinnacle Lake. Hiking around it definitely wasn't an option. Cliffs plunged directly down to the the shoreline at several different points. At others boulders and dense brush came to the water's edge.

Talk about the middle of nowhere! At least Lunker Lake had a bait shack and a few boats docked in the water. Here not a soul could be found. With Orville's truck gone, there wasn't a car or a person in sight.

"Good thing I found us a boat," Sam muttered.

"That's for sure," I agreed.

Sam began to load the Video Sub and TV into the boat along with the other equipment. When she finished, she spoke to Felix. "How do you feel now?"

"Not bad. Just give me a minute." Felix took a swig of water from his canteen. He paced back and forth, folding his arms around his stomach, encouraging it to settle down. Sam and I grabbed hold of the canoe and carried it toward the water.

"Are you sure this thing floats?" I asked with my teeth clenched. The canoe was heavy!

"I'm positive it *might*," Sam answered.

"Oh, that helps."

"Careful," Sam warned. We stepped over a log and around some large rocks. Pine needles formed a mat for our feet. I crunched through them toward the water. Soon the needles gave way to moist dirt mixed with sand. I searched the ground in front of me for the best places to walk. That's when my eyes noticed the one thing I had hoped *not* to find.

"Oh, no," I moaned. "Not again."

"What now, Willie?" Sam asked.

"Forget it. You don't want to know." We struggled and wobbled the rest of the way to the lake and dropped the bow of the canoe in the water. Then I led Sam back to the spot of my bleak discovery. Felix made his way over from the spot where Orville had dropped us off. I nodded toward the tire tracks in the mud. "Look familiar?"

"Don't tell me those are Scrub's," Felix said.

"He's here all right," I told them. "And even if we want to leave, we can't. Not with Orville gone for two hours."

Felix shook his head. "I don't think those are Scrub's tires. The treads on his truck were a different shape."

"There's one way to find out." I grabbed the Video Sub and asked Felix to remove the camera. He rewound to the spot where we had recorded the tire tracks at the bait shack, then hit play. We felt like detectives as we studied the videotape on the TV monitor.

"Convinced?" I asked, looking over at the tracks in the mud.

"Not really," Felix replied. "The video isn't zoomed in close enough to tell."

"Sam took it," I said. But seeing the concern in his eyes, and in Sam's, I wondered if I should have said anything. I was feeling kind of freaked out myself. I remembered the alligator and its rows of sharp teeth. "Well, whomever the tracks belong to, he's gone now," I said.

"You hope," Sam added. We weren't sure if we would feel safer in the boat or on dry land. At least in the boat we would be accomplishing our mission.

"Let's do it," I announced with a confident nod. With that we climbed in the canoe and shoved off through the blue mountain water to begin our surveillance. "Remember," I told them, "tough times don't last, but tough people do."

"Or to put it another way," Sam added, "I can do everything through Him who gives me strength."

"I think I like hers better," Felix said to me.

I agreed, though at the moment I felt more like the *Titanic* than a battleship going to war. Still, it felt pretty good to remember that Jesus was in the boat with us. He'd done some amazing things in boats!

Mrs. Crubble had been able to find only one paddle so we had to take turns using it. I was first and moved us away from shore with a few deep strokes. The water rippled with a late afternoon breeze. It was just enough to cool us down without tipping the canoe. When we were about 40 feet offshore, I rested the paddle across my knees.

Felix sat cross-legged in the front of the boat with the TV positioned on the seat so we could all see it. Sam sat in the middle. I sat in back.

"This looks good," Felix said. He pushed the record button on the camera, then lowered the Video Sub into the water. As the submarine dove deeper and deeper, Sam lowered cable over the side of the boat. Felix worked the remote control.

"Time to see what's down there," Felix said. He turned on the TV and we all watched closely.

"This is so cool," I said with enthusiasm. "Submarine surveillance at its finest." The depths opened before us on the TV screen. Because of the lake's rocky bottom and higher elevation, the visibility was much better than at Lunker Lake.

"Look at those plants," Sam said in wonder. "They're so lush and green."

"Yeah, just like Felix's face on the drive up here," I said. "You didn't go from carsick to seasick, did you, Super Sci?"

"Just keep us moving," Felix told me. "I'll be fine."

While paddling I kept a watchful eye on the TV screen. Sure the water was a gorgeous blue and the plants a rich green, but that's not what we had come to see. The big question still needed to be answered. Would this lake have fish in it or a poacher's net?

"There's a trout," Sam announced. "Follow it."

Using the remote, Felix turned the submarine after the fish. The live underwater view couldn't have been better. Now we knew exactly where to go.

Sam pointed at the TV. "Hurry! The trout's getting away."

Felix hit the throttle on the remote control. The Video Sub picked up speed and drew within a few feet of the trout's tail. We could see particles hitting the front window of the submarine, then sliding past. The cable whipped over the edge of the canoe into the water.

"Willie, you'd better hurry up. The Video Sub's getting away from us. We're running out of cable," Sam warned.

I paddled as fast as I could. My shoulders burned from the strain.

"Hurry!" Sam screamed.

The paddle splashed the water with each stroke. The submarine cruised ahead as Felix tried to keep up with the trout. He stared at the TV, oblivious to the problem. Cable loops flew over the side of the boat. With one end of the cable fastened to the Video Sub and the other to the TV, I knew what was coming.

"Sam, grab the TV!" I yelled between breaths.

"What?" she asked.

"The TV! Now!" The final loop of cable went over the edge. The line snapped tight and jerked the TV. It lifted off the bench and headed for the side of the canoe. Sam lunged.

"Got it!" she yelled.

"Yes!" I said, feeling relieved. Big mistake.

Wham! The canoe slammed into a boulder. I flew forward and my knees hit the middle seat. Clutching the TV, Sam lurched sideways toward the bow and almost into the water. Felix grabbed her before she went swimming.

"Way to go, Willie," Felix complained. "Learn to steer."

"Catch a clue," I shouted. "You're the one who almost sent the TV over the edge."

"You told me to keep up with the trout," he countered. "Why can't you row any faster?"

"I'm not rowing, I'm paddling."

"I'm not sure you're doing either," Felix replied.

We finished trading complaints and got organized again. Sam balanced the TV carefully on the front seat again. Felix maneuvered the Video Sub back beside the boat.

"From now on we stay under control," Felix said. "No more chasing fish. If they're out there, we'll see them. If not, we'll find the net soon enough."

I grabbed the paddle and got us moving again. Sam leaned over to rewind the cable, but something else caught her attention. She stared at the side of the canoe, frozen stiff.

"What's wrong, Sam?" I asked.

Her voice shook with fear, "What was the name of the bait shack guy again?"

"Scrub," I said.

"As in *S. Crubble*?" she asked. "Look what the first five letters spell."

I looked at the name etched in the side of the boat. "I d-d-don't b-b-believe it!" I stammered. But it was true. No wonder Scrub's name tag looked funny. He had removed the final three letters to create a nickname.

"What?" Felix wailed. "You borrowed Scrub's boat? The *poacher's* boat?"

"How was I supposed to know?" Sam demanded. Then she looked at me. "Willie, you didn't tell Scrub's wife where we were taking the boat, did you?"

I shrugged. "Maybe I sort of mentioned something about it."

Sam sighed. "Yep, I'd say those tire tracks were his," she said.

Felix just moaned, looking up to heaven. "Why me, Lord? Why me?"

"Now what do we do?" Sam asked.

"We keep searching for a net and hope Scrub's gone," I said. "Orville won't be back for more than an hour. There's no reason to just sit on shore and wait. We're just as safe out here as there." I tried to sound confident, but I felt anything but confident or *safe*, for that matter.

12

The Scuba Diver's Catch

We resumed our surveillance, but the lake didn't make for interesting viewing. The Video Sub kept an even pace beneath us but not a fish could be found. I stared at the screen, thinking a school of trout would swim by soon, or maybe a bass, but nothing did.

We were about to give up when a tail sliced through the water in front of the submarine. "What was that?" Sam asked.

"Follow it," I commanded Felix, not sure what I'd seen.

"Yeah, right," he said. "We're not doing that again."

"At least turn the sub so we can watch it," Sam said. Felix used the remote to turn the submarine. We stared at the screen. As the camera panned around, we saw nothing but blue.

"We must have lost it," I said. After searching a little more, we began to relax … too soon.

Suddenly, giant jaws and jagged rows of teeth charged the Video Sub. "The alligator!" we shrieked, expecting our vessel to get chomped. But the alligator turned into deeper water and disappeared.

"Now what?" Sam asked.

I had to tell her. "It could be getting up speed to charge us again."

Felix buried his face in his hands. "Just when you think it can't get any worse, it does."

Sam drew her hands inside the boat. I lifted the paddle into the air, ready to crack the alligator on the snout. We glanced nervously back and forth between the TV and the water, expecting an attack. But the alligator didn't return.

I dipped the paddle into the water, sending the canoe gliding along parallel to the shore. I was determined to find evidence that the warden could use. So far Scrub seemed like our number 1 suspect: first, no fish and now an alligator. Getting some videotape of the net would seal our case. Then we'd just have to find the game warden.

"What's that?" Sam asked. Silver outlines swerved in the water ahead.

"Right on schedule," I said. The scene on the TV looked just as it had when we'd found the net at Lunker Lake. "Now if we can just take a few shots of the net and get out of here alive."

The Video Sub moved in. The silver flashes took on shapes. Soon fish could be seen, snagged by their gills in the net.

"How terrible," Sam moaned.

"Now you know why the poacher didn't want us to come up here," I said. As we eased ahead we could see the top of the net. "Let's cruise along the net into deeper water to see where it goes," I suggested.

Felix turned the submarine and we followed along. Fish by the dozens hung in the net. They flipped frantically to get loose.

"What was that?" Sam asked, pointing at the TV screen.

"Normally, I'd say a fish," I told her. "But with an alligator swimming around, your guess is as good as mine."

"I don't think it was either," Felix said. "Row faster so we can find out."

"Aye, aye, captain," I said, leaning into the paddle.

Felix moved the Video Sub along the net, turning from side to side to search the water. We stared at the screen, ready for anything. Then we saw it again. A pair of black fins flipped into the depths. It was a person— a scuba diver! Felix maneuvered the submarine in pursuit.

"Don't get too close," I ordered. "That must be the poacher. This is our chance to catch him in the act."

The scuba diver reached the bottom. One by one he pulled fish from the net and stuffed them into a large bag tied to his waist.We watched in awe, not knowing what to do.

"It's got to be Scrub," I said. "He cleans the net while the alligator stands guard."

"Don't be so sure," Felix said.

"That's true, Willie," Sam agreed. "We haven't seen his face yet."

"And we won't with him wearing a scuba mask and hood. With all that gear hiding him, it could be any-body," Felix said.

"Then let's wait for him to finish. He has to surface sometime," I said. We positioned the canoe so we could keep an eye on the poacher without being dis-covered.

The poacher grabbed a fat trout by the back of the head and stuffed it into his bag. Soon his bag bulged with fish. With a strong pump of his fins, he pushed away from the net. He swam with long, even strokes for the other side of the lake.

We followed at a short distance, feeling like under-cover spies. Paddling carefully, I sent the canoe gliding silently across the water. I tried to figure out the poach-er's destination. On the shoreline across the lake, I spotted a break in the cliffs. Between two steep walls of rock, the bank sloped down to the water. Trees and boulders covered the area, offering plenty of places to hide a truck.

"Check out where the boulders come down to the lake," I whispered to Sam and Felix. "We can hide behind one of them and videotape the poacher getting out of the water."

"Sounds good," Sam said.

"Easy now. Don't let him see you," I cautioned Felix as he maneuvered the submarine.

"Just keep us moving. And try not to splash the water," he reminded me. I worked the paddle as best I could, but I was exhausted. We began to fall behind.

Felix opened the throttle on the remote, moving the Video Sub ahead to keep up with the poacher.

"Hurry, Willie! If the poacher gets to shore before we hide behind a boulder, he'll see us," Sam said. Then she took over so I could rest. She flipped the paddle from side to side like a pro.

"Nice work," Felix said.

"Now aren't you glad I'm on the flag team?" Sam asked with a smile. "This is just like waving a flag." Soon we caught up to the poacher. He kicked into shallow water with his bag full of fish in tow.

"That's far enough," Felix said. He brought the submarine around to the boat. Leaning over, I lifted it aboard.

Sam paddled us to a boulder that sat about four feet out of the water. We floated behind it, about 40 feet offshore—the perfect spot for surveillance.

"It's creepy not being able to see him," Felix said.

"No kidding," Sam added. "What if he turns back and charges our boat? We won't even see him coming."

We crouched down in the boat, hiding behind the boulder.

"Anytime, now," I mumbled, feeling tense. We watched the shore carefully. Ripples broke the surface.

"There!" I whispered. The scuba diver lifted his head from the water. He scouted the trees, then looked from side to side to make sure no one was watching him. Then he turned toward our boulder!

We ducked down. Holding our breath, we waited. We heard struggling in the water. I chanced a peek. The diver pulled himself out of the water and sat down on a log. Reaching down, he began to remove his swim fins.

"Quick!" I motioned to Felix, wanting the Video Sub. Raising it to my shoulder, I zoomed in on the scuba diver. I balanced carefully. The poacher looked around one more time, then removed his mask.

Like a Turbo Torpedo

My mouth fell open. I stared in awe, not sure I could believe my own eyes. "It isn't," I finally whispered.

"It is," Sam answered.

"The game warden?" Felix muttered, just as stunned.

After removing his scuba tank, the warden hoisted the heavy bag of fish over his shoulder. Then he turned to walk up the slope. I steadied the Video Sub on my shoulder, recording his every move. As the slope leveled out a little, the warden paused between some trees. He pulled a few branches aside and we could see his truck. He dumped the bag of fish into the storage bin in the truck bed. Then he grabbed something long and narrow with a canvas bag wrapped around it.

"What's that?" I wondered out loud.

The warden started back down the hill again. At the water's edge he put on his diving gear. He was preparing to swim out for another bag of fish. *The sooner the bet-*

ter, I thought, wanting him to submerge so we could leave. This time our videotape would go straight to the police.

Then my hand slipped. The submarine knocked into the boulder sheltering us with a bump that echoed across the lake. We ducked down as fast as we could. We heard splashes in the water, then silence. A few moments passed. Still no sound. I had to look. Lifting my head, I peeked toward shore. The warden was gone.

"Let's get out of here," I said.

Sam dug deep with the paddle. Felix lowered the Video Sub into the water to try and find the poacher. It darted back and forth beneath the boat, recording everything in its path. Soon we reached the middle of the lake.

"You can slow down now," I told Sam, convinced the poacher was far behind.

Working the remote, Felix turned the submarine around. Nothing. He moved the controls, making the sub climb and dive. Still nothing. As a final attempt, he tried turning the Video Sub back in the direction we were heading.

"Arghh!" we screamed in unison. The poacher's face filled the TV screen! He was swimming for the submarine, glaring at the camera.

"Mayday! Mayday!" I shouted. "Reverse! Now!"

"I'll take care of the Video Sub," Felix shouted. "You just get us out of here." Felix backed the Video Sub away from the game warden, keeping the camera lens focused on his face. I grabbed the paddle from Sam and drove it into the water.

"What's he doing now?" I asked, straining to stroke the paddle with all my strength.

"He's unwrapping that long cylinder. The one covered by the bag," Felix said, studying the screen.

"What is it?" I asked.

"Oh, no, not that," Felix moaned.

"What?" I demanded.

Felix shook his head. "You don't want to know."

"I don't want to be here either, but that's beside the point," I said. "What is it?"

"It's a speargun," Felix told us.

"What!" I leaned forward and studied the screen. I felt the blood drain from my face. "That's not a speargun. That's a spear *cannon*! It'll blow a hole right through our submarine and our camera."

"Don't worry," Felix assured me. "He's not aiming at the Video Sub."

"What's he aiming at?" Sam asked.

"Us," Felix yelled. "*Fire one!*" Seconds later a spearhead pierced the bottom of the canoe, just inches from my foot. Water poured in around the shaft.

"Man the pumps!" Sam ordered.

Felix looked around. "What pumps? We don't have any pumps. Just get us to shore."

I started to aim for the spot where Orville would pick us up, but I realized we'd never make it in time. Our only hope was to loop back to the bank below the warden's truck. I paddled as fast as I could, desperate to get away from the poacher, but he was gaining on us. He surfaced and stroked the top of the water like an Olympic swimmer.

Water continued to seep in around the spear and fill the boat. Felix maneuvered the Video Sub back to the boat, then brought it aboard. I gave the paddle back to Sam. She dug and pulled with all her might.

"Sam, you're not related to Pocahontas, are you?" I asked.

"I told you, it's just like flag practice," she said, putting a little distance between us and the poacher. But with so much water filling the canoe, it didn't last. The warden kicked hard and strong, pushing closer with each thrust of his fins. He was 20 feet away. Fifteen.

"Hurry," Felix told us.

Sam dug deep with the paddle, straining with all her might. But the boat continued to take on water. Then I remembered our earlier episode and what the submarine could do. "Felix, launch the submarine," I ordered. "We need a tow. Now!"

Felix grabbed the cable and powered the submarine straight ahead. "Hang on, guys!" The poacher closed in. Ten feet away. Five. He reached for the boat.

The cable grew taunt. Felix hit the turbo switch. "We have liftoff," he announced.

The Video Sub shot forward like a torpedo. The canoe lunged forward. Our heads snapped back. Whiplash!

"Yes!" I shouted as the wind whipped my hair.

The game warden reloaded his speargun and took another shot. Not even close. As he faded behind us, Sam pulled in the paddle and relaxed. She deserved it. If it hadn't been for her, the poacher would have caught us for sure. Felix remained at the helm, using the remote to guide us to the poacher's landing spot.

"Are you sure we can't make it to Orville?" Sam asked.

"Positive. We're taking on too much water," Felix said.

He was right. The boat continued to leak. Soon the submarine labored to keep us moving. At about 50 feet from shore, it gave out. The batteries were dead. Grabbing the oar, I forced the boat into about three feet of water. We jumped out just before it sank.

"Get the Video Sub!" I told Felix. As I grabbed the TV, I worked to steady my feet on the slippery mud bottom. Then I remembered the alligator. What if Molly showed up for a late afternoon kid snack?

Felix and Sam waded toward shore ahead of me. I followed, hoping to make it to dry ground. Farther out the warden lifted his head out of the water. I imagined I could see the fury in his eyes.

Teetering back and forth, I wobbled to shore with the TV. Felix and Sam scrambled up the bank with me close behind. Clutching boulders and branches, we made our way up the hill. As the warden reached the boat, it sank completely.

Pushing ahead, we neared the green truck and checked the ignition. "If only the warden had left the keys," I moaned.

"If only one of us knew how to drive," Sam added.

"Good point," I said as we took off. We followed a dirt path that led through the trees. It led us to a plateau above the cliffs. At the top we paused to look back. The warden stood at the water's edge, taking off his fins.

Felix calculated the distance between us. We had to get to Orville before the warden got to us. "I think we can make it," he said.

With the submarine, cable, and TV still connected, the three of us ran together. Water squished from our tennis shoes. Pine needles crunched under our feet.

We worked our way along the plateau high above the lake, dodging branches, pushing through brush that scratched our skin. Our legs felt like flimsy rubber, but we kept going.

"Closer to the edge," I said, directing our path. I wanted to keep an eye on the lake, just in case Orville showed up early. But the key was not getting too close to the edge.

"Look out!" Sam shouted. Her feet slipped over into nothingness. She clawed at the ground.

"Hold on to the cable," I told her. I grabbed a branch and set my feet against a rock.

Felix jumped behind a tree with the Video Sub.

Sam caught a clump of grass and tried to stop. But it was too late.

14

A Video Sub Sandwich

The grass roots tore loose in Sam's hand. She plunged over the cliff. "The cable!" I shouted, watching her disappear.

We waited. Hoping. Praying. Suddenly, the cable grew taunt. It jerked hard against our hands, but we held on.

"Sam?" Felix yelled. No answer.

"Sam?" I shouted.

"I'm okay," she replied.

"Thank You, Lord," I whispered in relief. Then I explained my plan to Felix. "Ready?" He nodded.

We carefully brought up the cable. First, I pulled my end. Then, while I rested, Felix pulled his end. We went back and forth. Our hands burned and our arms ached, but we kept pulling.

"Sam?" I called. "Are you almost to the top?"

Silence. My stomach felt sick. If anything happened to her … Sam's fingers lifted above the ledge, still clutching the cable. Then the top of her head came into view. We pulled her the rest of the way, then gave her a hug. Collapsing on the ground, we stared up at the blue sky. I knew each one of us was sending a silent thank You to God.

Then a terrible and familiar sound cut short our celebration. A truck's engine rumbled behind us.

"The game warden!" I said, remembering our predicament. He had reached his truck and was continuing to pursue us. We had to keep going. The spot where we were going to meet Orville was close. I checked my watch. He should arrive any minute. We gathered our equipment and started to run.

The warden's truck closed in behind us. We pushed ahead, this time keeping our distance from the edge of the cliff. Twigs scraped against our legs. We gasped for air.

"I've had enough," Felix moaned. But Sam and I spurred him on. We made it to the end of the cliffs. The land sloped toward the lake again. Jumping from the dirt path, we made our way through the thick trees, knowing the truck couldn't follow us. We were right. Soon we heard the truck stop and a door open, followed by footsteps crunching through the underbrush.

Pain cut through my side, but I kept running, clutching the small TV. I stayed in front, followed by Sam. Felix remained in the back, pulled by the cable attached to the Video Sub. Then the sound of another truck hit us. But this one was in front of us. I knew the low rumble right away. It belonged to Scrub.

"No, it can't be!" I wailed.

"What?" Felix gasped between breaths.

"The warden and Scrub are in this together," I said, thinking I had finally solved the mystery. "And we're sandwiched between them."

The rumble of the truck's engine grew louder, echoing off the water. We kept running. We entered a clearing bordered on one side by thick trees. Maybe we could sneak past Scrub and make it to Orville.

Wrong again. Scrub's truck burst into the clearing and stopped. The alligator slid off the bed and clawed the ground, preparing to pounce.

I dug in my feet and fell backward, but Sam and Felix were still moving forward. We collided and crumbled to the ground. Just then the warden burst through the trees behind us. The alligator charged, her mouth open and teeth dripping.

I lifted the TV over my head in defense, ready to bring it crashing down like a hammer. But I didn't need to. I stared in awe as the alligator ran right past us. She went for the game warden. We all turned to watch.

The warden aimed his speargun and fired. The spear shot toward the alligator, then curved and missed! Molly bore down, not at all happy with the warden. He turned and ran. He made it to a tree and jumped for a branch just as the alligator chomped.

"Yeow!" the warden yelled as Molly tore a piece of wet suit from his seat. Still too petrified to move, Felix, Sam, and I watched in horror, not knowing if we were safe or the alligator's next meal. Orville's arrival answered that question. He rushed into the clearing with two police officers.

"It's about time you showed up," Scrub said to the officers. "Molly, get over here." The alligator quickly tromped back to Scrub's side.

The officers pulled the warden out of the tree and handcuffed him. After putting him in the squad car, they checked on us to make sure we were okay. We were still too stunned to speak. We just nodded.

Orville came over and explained what he could. "Scrub sent me for the police when he saw what was happening."

"But he's the poacher," I protested.

"The poacher?" Scrub asked, then laughed. "Now how's that for gratitude."

Nothing made sense to me. "But what about the alligator and the warnings for us to stay away?"

Scrub shrugged. "I didn't want you to get hurt. That's why I kept an eye on you."

"So you knew the warden was the poacher all along?" I asked.

"No. But I had my suspicions. That's when I brought Molly to the bait shack for protection. Before all this I just kept her in the pond at my house."

Felix held the Video Sub under his arm like a football. With the record button still on, he had captured everything, and everyone, on film.

"Good thing you borrowed my canoe," Scrub said. "I knew just where to look for you."

I started to apologize. "Oh, about your boat ..."

"Don't worry about it," Scrub interrupted. "I've patched the thing before. I can patch it again."

By now I was speechless. Scrub still had bug eyes, wiry whiskers, and one long eyebrow that looked like a flat Tootsie Roll. But so what? He had saved my skin once again. So much for judging by appearances.

"You're all to be commended," the senior police officer announced. "Your surveillance work was excellent." He walked over and eyed our submarine. "By the way, what's with the torpedo toaster?"

"Not again," I moaned, shaking my head.

Felix shrugged. "Willie designed it. I just made it work."

Everyone enjoyed the laugh, and this time, I didn't even care if it was on me.

15

Willie's Last Laugh

Sitting in a front seat in the Washington Elementary auditorium, I felt nervous. Sam's parents were sitting a few seats over from me. Mr. Stewart looked impatient.

Sam's flag team was about to perform. When they'd won the fall invitational, the principal of the elementary school had asked them to give a special victory performance.

Suddenly, music blasted from speakers and echoed off the wood floor. The team marched across the gym in the shape of an arrow. Sam led the way.

At Sam's signal the girls waved their flags in perfect unison, bringing them up and down like clockwork. They marched quickly in place and forward and backward. With each beat, they twirled their flags, and themselves, with perfect grace.

For a grand finale the flag team formed the letter *W* for Washington Elementary. That brought everyone to their feet, including Mr. Stewart. He cheered louder than anyone.

Sam beamed with delight, and so did I, knowing how much she had wanted her dad's support. She came over and gave him a hug, then sat down next to Felix. Looking around, I noticed more smiles of approval from grandparents, children, even Crusher Grubb.

"Crusher Grubb!" I blurted out. "What's *he* doing here?"

Felix gave me a worried look. "If he sees that video of us in skirts, we're history."

I gulped, painfully reminded of what would follow. For the final presentation of the day, Phoebe was about to show her video of "someone admirable"— me.

It was bad enough to have Crusher Grubb in the audience, but the presentations about the other admired people made me feel worse. One was a doctor; the other was the founder of a shelter for the homeless. Those choices made sense considering how much they did to help people. But me?

Mrs. Hedger, Phoebe's teacher, walked on stage. "Our next presentation is by Phoebe Synder."

Phoebe walked to the podium, cleared her throat, and began. "Honorary guests, faculty, and fellow students, the person I admire attended Washington Elementary just a few years ago. He is none other than Willie Plummet." She paused as if expecting a round of applause.

I didn't know what to expect, but just to be safe, I ducked a little lower in my seat. Not that I had graduated on bad terms. Let's just say you can break only so many windows, set off only so many fire alarms, and spill only so many gallons of finger paint before ruffling a few feathers. The truth is I did more than ruffle a few feathers, I plucked the bird.

I looked up. The auditorium still had chocolate fragments on the ceiling from my candy volcano eruption. I noticed the biggest blob right above the spot where Phoebe was standing. "Great," I groaned, feeling the heat. Then I started to pray. "Lord, please don't let it drop on Phoebe now."

"Without further ado," Phoebe continued, "I give you *Willie Plummet's Fall Break.*"

One look at the opening sequence and I wanted to hide. It began with me in my mom's pink robe, followed by me in my Pooh Bear pajamas on Phoebe's front porch. The auditorium roared with laughter. The teachers laughed the loudest, as if they were finally getting even.

I sank down in my seat and closed my eyes. My face felt redder than my hair. I couldn't stand to watch. Great. All my most embarrassing moments enlarged on the big screen. What scene would be next? Me as a giant chicken, half-covered with spit up? Talking with a chunk of spinach in my teeth? Swishing from side to side in a glittery gold skirt? No doubt they'd roar at how ridiculous I looked. I covered my ears, anticipating the laugher.

But it never came.

I cracked open an eyelid. It was a shot from the Video Sub when we'd first found the net at Lunker Lake. Then the entire mystery began to unfold on the screen. The second trip to Lunker Lake. My commitment to find the truth. Scrub's tire tracks. Phoebe presented a play-by-play narration of how we'd solved the crime.

"This is awesome," a voice behind me whispered.

"Totally," another kid replied.

I looked around. Everyone in the auditorium was staring at the screen in awe, eating it up. Even Crusher Grubb sat forward in his seat, mouth hanging open.

More scenes added detail to the story. Felix, Sam, and I working and planning in the lab. Adding a "live" feed to the Video Sub. Launching the canoe at Pinnacle Lake. The alligator charging the sub. Kids screamed as if Molly was coming right at them.

Then there came the net full of fish. The scuba diver. The speargun blasting through our boat. Even the warden chasing us along the trail was on film. Then I remembered that Felix had left the camera on *record*. In all the hysteria, I had forgotten about it. On screen we climbed the hill, ran along the cliff, and Sam fell!

The audience shuddered with fear. We pulled Sam back. Then we entered the clearing. Then Scrub. The alligator. The warden. The police. Orville. The end.

I sat in my seat, stunned. Seeing it all on screen emphasized what a great job God had done to keep us safe. But if He loved us enough to have given His Son's life for us, He has to love us enough to watch over us. Then I noticed Phoebe smiling at the audience. "Please join me in honoring the brave crook-catcher himself, Willie Plummet!"

Cheers and applause filled the auditorium. I couldn't believe it. They didn't care about how I'd looked in the pink robe or the Pooh Bear pajamas. They thought I'd accomplished something pretty incredible.

Phoebe waved me to the stage. I shook my head no, but she came down and pulled my hand. Standing up, I dragged Sam and Felix to the stage with me. As we got to the podium, the crowd gave us a standing ovation.

"You're the best, Phoebe," I told her, giving her a high five.

"No, you are," she said, pushing the microphone in front of my face.

"First, I'd like to thank God for taking care of us and for helping us bring the poacher to justice," I said. "We couldn't have done a thing on our own. Next, I'd like to thank my two best friends, Felix and Sam. They always stood by me, even when it would have been easy to call it quits. And thanks to Phoebe too. Without her camera, we wouldn't have found the net."

With my arms thrown across their shoulders, Felix, Sam, Phoebe, and I took a bow. Then, after a quick glance at the ceiling, we hurried off the stage before chocolate rained down on our parade.

1 — the misadventures of Willie Plummet ① — **INVASION from planet X** — BUCHANAN & RANDALL

2 — the misadventures of Willie Plummet ② — **submarine SANDWICHED** — BUCHANAN & RANDALL

3 — the misadventures of Willie Plummet ③ — **ANYTHING you can do I can do BETTER** — BUCHANAN & RANDALL

4 — the misadventures of Willie Plummet ④ — **ballistic BUGS** — BUCHANAN & RANDALL

5 — the misadventures of Willie Plummet ⑤ — **battle of the BANDS** — BUCHANAN & RANDALL

6 — the misadventures of Willie Plummet ⑥ — **Gold Flakes for Breakfast** — BUCHANAN & RANDALL

Look for all these **exciting** WiLLiE PLuMMeT misadventures at your local Christian bookstore!